Dragon Fire
O C E A N   M I S T

Yvonne Palka

Published by
HeartRock Press
P.O. Box 135
Langley, WA 98260

FIRST EDITION

Cover and Interior Design by Yachun Peng
Illustrations by Yvonne Palka
Calligraphy by Chizue Rudd

Library of Congress Cataloging-in-Publication Data
Yvonne Palka.
Dragon Fire, Ocean Mist / by Yvonne Palka.
13-digit ISBN 978-0-9817668-0-5
10-digit ISBN 0-9817668-0-3

1. Dragons-Fiction 2. Fantasy
I. Title: Dragon Fire, Ocean Mist

To my granchildren who inspired these stories

and to all children everywhere

May you discover the joy that lives

in your own hearts

CONTENTS

"Whooee!" shouted Jaxon, as he and his sister were swept up over the tops of the tall firs. "Hey, Allie, can you see Dad and Mom down there? They're tiny, like ants!" He was holding on to a spike with one arm and pointing below them with the other.

"Hang on, Jaxon!" Allie, breathless with excitement, hugged tightly to the spike of the great creature she was riding. The salt air scrubbed her face, and she could see how the setting sun made Jaxon's cheeks glow. Then she noticed the eagle.

"Wow. Look over there, Jaxon—we're eye to eye with that eagle." Jaxon looked and sure enough, there was an eagle just off to the right, eyeing them cautiously as the serpentine shapes glided past.

The two giant creatures soon left the eagle behind as they swooped and curved around the sea stacks just off the edge of Shi Shi Beach. From that great height the cresting waves looked small, too, but Jaxon and Allie knew from past visits that those rollers were much larger than they appeared. Then the race was on!

"Come on, Shiran, how high can we climb?" Jaxon hollered. He grabbed the spike with both hands as the great beast pulled into a powerful arc skyward. Allie, too, rose gracefully away from the ground far below, her hair streaming.

Side by side the two creatures and their human companions rose, until they were looking down at the tops of the tall firs that guarded the cliff edge. "Hey, Allie, this must be how the astronauts feel when they rocket away from earth!" Jaxon shouted.

Allie just shook her head. How could he talk so much when she couldn't even catch her breath? That crazy brother! They cruised and glided high over the trees and above Shi Shi Beach.

Then, all too soon, the four, beasts and children, found themselves heading back down to the sand. With a flap of powerful wings and one twist of a long sinuous tail, each massive creature landed gently at the water's edge. This incredible ride was over.

Allie rubbed the sleek neck of her hostess, Shalini. "Thank you," she said, and the stars in the creature's eyes shone even brighter.

Jaxon slid down reluctantly from the back of his companion and looked back up in awe. "You're so cool," he said.

one DRAGON BACK ROCKS

Jaxon and Allie were camping with their parents for a week on Shi Shi Beach on the Washington coast. (While hiking in they'd chanted the name, *Shy, Shy,* in excitement.) They loved camping on the sand, cooking over the campfire, and sleeping out under the stars. But most of all they loved exploring and having adventures.

As Jaxon and Allie approached the Point of the Arches at the south end of Shi Shi beach, they caught sight of the familiar rows of small pointed rocks lined up neatly one after the other in the sand, pointing in an arc out to the sea. Jaxon and Allie had their own name for these rocks. They called these the Dragon Back Rocks, like the spikes on a dragon's back. Now, as the two gazed out at them, Jaxon said, "You know, they really just look like rocks." He let his soccer ball drop to the sand and kicked it a little ways.

"C'mon, Jaxon, remember what happened last year!" said Allie. "There's no way you could forget that ride we took!" She looked hard at her brother. "We just have to climb up on the big log and wait!" He knew as well as she did what they'd seen. Why was he acting this way?

"Yeah, I remember. But look—it's just rocks with a lot of seaweed hanging off of them. Maybe that's all they are."

"No, we just have to be patient," said Allie. The year before, sitting on the big log, Jaxon and Allie had made the most amazing discovery of their lives. They'd waited all through the rains of last winter for another chance to see if it would happen again. Finally the time was almost here.

"Okay," Jaxon grumbled. He didn't like to wait but he knew his sister was right. They climbed up onto the smaller end of the huge log and balanced their way down to the big end near the thick tangle of roots. Allie found a comfortable spot to sit. She took the sketchbook and colored pencils that traveled with her everywhere, and began drawing the rows and rows of Dragon Back Rocks.

The drawing would make the perfect basis for a sumi-e painting when she got back to camp. Snugging his favorite soccer cap firmly on his head, Jaxon jumped down onto the sand in front of Allie and began practicing different moves with his soccer ball.

A few minutes later, just as Allie was putting a final stroke on her first picture, it was spattered with a spray of damp sand. "Jaxon!" she cried. "Why can't you watch what you're doing with that stupid ball!" She looked in dismay at the ruined sketch.

"Oops, sorry," said her brother, but he didn't look very sorry. Instead he kept on, trying to move the ball in an arc the way he'd seen his favorite players do so well. Allie glared at him. "Watch this, Allie," he said. "They call this the banana kick."

"You're the one who's gone bananas," she said, rolling her eyes, but he just grinned at her and kept trying the new move. Then she noticed some sticky chocolate on Jaxon's chin from the s'mores they'd had for dessert back in camp. Allie laughed.

"What? What's so funny?" said Jaxon, touching his face where his sister was pointing. His hand came away sticky with marshmallow and chocolate.

They were abruptly interrupted by a faint rumbling. Allie tucked away her pencils. Jaxon scrambled back up onto the log and set aside his soccer ball. As the children watched, the sand gradually began to move in small waves, until the log they were sitting on began to rock back and forth. The pointed rocks began to move, just a little at first. Brother and sister looked at each other, eyes wide. They didn't dare move. The trembling of the beach made the log shift to one side, and in one motion both Jaxon and Allie reached over to grab a handful of roots for support. Slowly, like a rising island, a giant body began to emerge from the sand. After a long moment, a large blue head lifted up and looked around sleepily.

"Look, it's Shiran!" Allie squealed.

Jaxon couldn't find any words. But he nodded at his sister and held tight to the root. So they weren't just rocks! Last summer wasn't just in his imagination!

Sure enough, there was Shiran the great dragon, in all his glorious scales and spikes, shaking the sand off his enormous blue body. He was as big as a school bus, but curved and sleek, the spikes along his back a dusky pink. In the fading light his scales seemed alive, throwing off iridescent flashes of color. In broad daylight he was bright blue, but now, as the sun began to set, Shiran's body shimmered with flashes of pink and orange. The children later discovered that sometimes when the fog and mist came in across Shi Shi, the huge dragon's scales shone with a soft blue-green like the sea. Shiran's eyes were wise but fierce. And those eyes often twinkled, especially when fire-fishing or new adventures with children were at hand. Atop his immense head were two powerful, curved horns, smoothed and worn from the many years he'd been fishing and living in the caves of Shi Shi.

As Allie and Jaxon watched, Shiran slowly unfolded his wings and shook the sand out of the folds of wing-skin. With one hot blast he blew smoke and steam from his nostrils, so thick that for a moment his feet were hidden from view. His power and beauty mesmerized the children. They were so entranced they didn't see that someone else, nearly as big, was beginning to emerge from the sand nearby.

Then Jaxon turned. "Look, that must be Shalini!" he whispered. "Remember her?"

How could Allie forget? Shalini was the one who had taken them fire-fishing. Allie still got shivers of excitement when she thought about that amazing ride.

Shalini shook the sand off her head, then unfolded and spread her wings. Her scales were a deep magenta pink, and a row of vivid blue spikes went all the way down to the tip of her tail. Allie had dreamed about Shalini, and how she blended in so well with a Pacific beach sunset, when her scales would glitter with hints of green and flashes of gold. Her forehead had a small bump in the middle, and two small, tightly spiraled horns stood just in front of her large, soft ears. It was remarkable how delicate Shalini looked, but Allie knew she was strong and agile, too.

The magenta dragon's manner was kind and tender, especially when she looked at the children. When she spoke to them, her ears often flicked gently back and forth. And when the fog rolled in, Shalini loved to blow steam curls from her nostrils. Her steam curls would rise and blend with the fog, then gradually disappear altogether. It was Shalini's way of painting, Allie thought.

Shiran and Shalini stood up to their full height and stretched out their wings. Tip to tip, Shiran's wingspan was a good 30 feet wide, and he towered over the children. Shalini arched her neck, turning her head this way and that, gazing thoughtfully about as if seeing Shi Shi for the first time. "It feels good to be up and about again," she said to her mate. Jaxon and Allie couldn't explain quite how it was they could understand the two huge dragons. To any other listener the conversation might have sounded like nothing more than a series of high-pitched squeaks, squeals, and low, deep growls. But to the children every word was crystal clear.

Jaxon and Allie felt a sudden rush of air as the two dragons spread their immense wings and rose suddenly into the sky. They flew one after the other in a long, lazy circle just above where the children sat watching, eyes wide.

As the two dragons made a second pass overhead, Shalini spotted Jaxon and Allie. She landed and approached them.

"How delightful to see you again! We so enjoyed your company last summer," she exclaimed. "And we have someone we'd like you to meet!" With that, Shalini lowered her head toward two shorter rows of rocks. She made a long, low sound that sounded to Allie like a cat purring.

Jaxon and Allie watched as the sand around this row of rocks began to tremble. A few shivers and shakes later, a small, brilliant green dragon emerged. His spikes were bright orange-red. His scales didn't shimmer yet (that wouldn't happen until he was at least 100 years old). He was a noisy young fellow, they soon discovered—when he wanted to say something, he stretched his little body and let out a shrill, trumpeting sound. It was as if he was trying to roar, and Jaxon couldn't help but smile. He turned toward the children with a serious glare, and his rubbery spikes wobbled a bit. Allie giggled, and quickly clapped her hand over her mouth.

Shalini repeated her coaxing sounds until another small dragon, this one with purple scales and golden-yellow spikes, slowly emerged and shook the sand out of her wings. The purple she-dragon flipped her tail around and gave the green fellow a playful swat. He lurched toward her. The game was on! Back and forth they lunged at each other, wings wide, the purple one ducking elegantly out of the way as the little green fellow trumpeted in protest. Jaxon and Allie could feel the wind on their faces as the two dragons swooped back and forth.

"They've got to be brother and sister!" Jaxon whispered to Allie.

"What makes you say that?" Allie grinned and gave her brother a playful shove.

Shalini arched her neck and stood fully upright. One steam ring wafted into the air, and she said, "Now, Shoram, Shyla . . ." The small dragons took one last swipe at each other and turned toward their mother, who continued.

"I'd like you to meet Jaxon." She motioned gracefully with her huge head. "And Allie."

"Hey there," said Jaxon.

"Pleased to meet you," said Allie. Their voices sounded small after all the trumpeting. Then Jaxon just had to ask, "Which one of you is Shoram and which is Shyla?"

At that Shoram trumpeted, "I am mother smiled. stamped his front feet and Shoram the Fierce." His

And Shyla added, "I'm Shyla—I'm purple," she said, flipping her tail around in a cute little arc.

Allie said, "Hi, Shyla."

"Hi, Allie." Shyla paused

for a minute, then said, "I've never met a human before."
She sat silently watching the girl and then blurted, "Do
you like to go swimming underwater and catch fish and
eat them?"

Allie said, "Oh,
I love to swim, and
I can swim
underwater
for a little
while. And I like
to fish with my
Dad, and cook the fish over a
fire for dinner. But I didn't bring my fishing rod . . ."
She tried to picture this delicate little purple dragon
reeling in a fish.

"That's all right," said Shyla, flicking her tail. "We'll show
you how dragons fish."

At this Shoram jumped in and trumpeted, "Yes, we'll take you fishing! Right now! I'm hungry! Want to come, Jaxon?"

Jaxon was all set to say, "Sure," when Shalini interrupted gently. "I think it's best if we take Jaxon and Allie fishing tomorrow when we can all dry off in the sunshine afterward. The sun's nearly down now and it will soon be chilly. Shoram and Shyla, you can go now and catch your dinner if you wish."

At that Shoram and Shyla headed for the water, half flying and half hopping, racing to be first. Soon they had disappeared completely beneath the waves. The adult dragons turned to Jaxon and Allie. Shalini said, "We have something else we must tell you. There have been unfortunate changes on the beach since you were last here."

Jaxon and Allie listened as Shiran explained. "There's a family of difficult dragons that has claimed a cave on a beach close to Shi Shi. The parents are called Zorg and Zorgina, and they have one dragon boy-child, Zonta. We must caution you especially about Zorg." Allie looked at

Jaxon, who sat up a little straighter as Shiran continued the warning.

"Zorg comes around every so often to steal the fish we catch for our dinner. He seems to enjoy causing trouble. He frightens the seagulls by strolling up close and then roaring fire at them."

"And then he taunts them as they scatter away," Shalini added in dismay. "They try to escape without their feathers getting burned. He even knocks the gulls' nests down from the rocks during the breeding season." Her eyes were sad as she described the squawking, frightened seabirds. Allie wondered if perhaps that was why the gulls sounded so often like they were crying.

Shiran continued, "We haven't seen much of Zorgina or Zonta, but I have a feeling they're a great deal like Zorg. They aren't the tidy sort, anyway." He paused and smiled briefly. "Shoram and Shyla call their beach Stinky Fish Beach. No doubt you can guess why."

"We wanted you to know about these dragons

in case you see them. If they're approaching Shi Shi, you can be sure they're up to no good. So you must do all you can to stay out of their way, my friends." Shiran finished the story with a somber nod of his head.

Jaxon and Allie took in all this news very thoughtfully. Clearly it was a good idea to avoid these difficult dragons. In spite of his curiosity about how a really mean dragon would look and act, Jaxon said, "Okay, we'll watch out for them."

"Yes," said Allie. "Thanks for the warning."

Shalini nodded gravely at the two young humans, then looked up and saw that the sun was setting. "You two had better get back to your camp. I'll bet your parents are looking for you. Do please come back tomorrow during the daytime and we'll have an adventure!" And she lowered her big magenta head toward the children, looking tenderly at them with melting brown eyes. Her ears flicked gently as the two waved and headed back down the length of the log.

Jaxon and Allie looked back at Shalini and Shiran from the log. "See you tomorrow," they called, and waved goodbye. As they walked back to camp, Jaxon had all sorts of questions.

"How old do you think those dragons are, Allie? Where do they come from?" he asked.

But Allie didn't answer her brother, because a drawing was unfolding in her mind. How much fun it would be to try to paint the amazing colors of each dragon! She saw the many brilliant colors of the dragons flashing and changing in the setting sun. Suddenly Jaxon bumped into his sister. "Race you back to camp!" he yelled, as he ran ahead. "Bet I get there first!"

two FIRE-FISHING

The next day dawned bright and clear. Jaxon and Allie were eager to get back to the dragons. Their parents hadn't had their second cup of coffee yet when the children asked, "Is it okay if we go exploring in the tide pools down by the arches?"

Mom replied, "Sure. Just be careful to watch for the incoming tide so you don't get stranded somewhere when the water's too deep to get back. And don't go around the point to the next beach, all right?"

"We promise," said Jaxon. They immediately thought of Shiran's warning about Zorg, and knew they'd stay where their mother wanted them to be.

Eager to find their friends, Jaxon and Allie ran down

the beach. Both secretly wondered if the dragons would appear again. When they reached the Dragon Back Rocks, the two climbed up on the magic log and looked far out to sea. After a while they moved down a bit and sat on the big end near the huge tree's roots, but still nothing happened. No dragons.

"Where are they?" Allie moped.

"I dunno," Jaxon replied. "Maybe they're still asleep and we'll have to come back later. Let's look around for dragon tracks or dragon egg shells. Maybe we'll see something that other dragon, Zorg, left here. That'd be so cool!"

"Yeah, and those colored rocks Dad told us about?" Allie asked. "Where did those red ones come from? Do you remember, Jaxon?"

"Um, I think Dad said they're from Canada. They're jasper, I think. That'd be cool, to find some of them."

So that was just what they decided to try. Jaxon and Allie climbed down from the log and began to explore the sand that stretched from the cliffs to the cresting waves. Soon they were at the tide pools carved in the rocks at the base of the arches. The tide was going out and the rocks were covered with beautiful orange and purple sea stars. In the deep, shady pools they found lots of the big blue-green sea anemones, open like beautiful flowers. Iridescent dark red seaweed floated around the pool's edges. Allie sat down, got out her colored pencils, and began to draw. Purple, blue-green, orange, deep red—the tide pool reminded her of a rainbow.

Jaxon was entranced with the many hermit crabs scuttling back and forth across the sandy bottom. How did they get inside those snail shells? He caught one and put it on the sand, hoping it would run around his feet. But the tiny creature quickly tucked itself deep inside its shell. Only when Jaxon put it back into the shelter of the tide pool did the crab venture back out. Jaxon poked at some limpets, the small conical shellfish that couldn't be pried loose from the rocks.

But no dragon bones. Jaxon kept looking, turning over rocks to see what might be underneath. He wasn't sure what a dragon bone might look like, exactly, but he was certain he would know it when he saw one. As he searched, Jaxon was careful to turn the rocks back over to their original positions, so the animals living underneath would survive.

Then, half hidden beneath an algae-covered rock too big to move, Jaxon saw something whitish-yellow, an unusual color in the dark tones of the tide pools. He dug in the sand around its base to dislodge it from its resting place. When he had rinsed the sand off his discovery, he held it up to study. A round, disk-like object with three jagged protrusions around its edge, it covered most of his palm. The surface was hard and had millions of tiny dimples.

"Look at this, Allie!" he said. "This isn't a rock, or a shell either. Do you think it could be a piece of dragon bone?" Jaxon pictured himself loaded with an archeologist's gear, discovering evidence of ancient and mythical creatures.

"Oh sure, Jaxon." Allie sounded scornful, but she studied the item closely and finally shrugged her shoulders. "I guess you're right, it doesn't look like a shell or rock. Let's see what Dad says." Jaxon put the heavy piece in his deepest pocket and continued to explore.

The sun swung higher in the sky. Allie and Jaxon were so intent on exploring and drawing that they only realized what time it was when Allie said, "Wow. I'm really hungry." They both lurched up at once, and raced back to camp for lunch.

Over a lunch of sandwiches and apples, they shared their morning adventures with their parents. Jaxon pulled out the mystery bone from his pocket. "Do you know what this is?" he asked, handing it to his dad. Dad was a biologist and knew a lot about the natural history of the coast. Jaxon waited, hoping his father would be able to identify his odd find.

Dad studied it for a while, turning it over and over in his hands. "*Hmm*," he said. "I've never seen anything quite like it before. I'll ask some of my friends at the college when we get home. Maybe it's a fossil of some sort." Now Jaxon was even more excited to get back to the arches. No telling what else might be hidden out there!

Later in the afternoon Allie and Jaxon took off down the beach again, soccer ball and sketchpad in hand, in hopes of finding the real dragons. In no time they found their favorite seat on the magic log. But Jaxon was soon down on the sand again, this time practicing head shots with his soccer ball. Allie glared at him. "Don't you dare get sand all over me again, Jaxon. I mean it."

He grinned up at her. "Too bad there aren't any banana slugs on the beach," he teased. "One of those would really add something to your artwork." Allie loved to find and watch the slow, slimy yellow slugs, but she was glad there weren't any around just then. She scowled at her brother and chose a vivid blue color for her first drawing.

After a few minutes Jaxon rejoined his sister on the log, and sure enough, they soon saw Shiran and Shalini emerging from some deep caves just offshore in the arches. Right after them came Shoram and Shyla, gliding effortlessly from another smaller cave closer to shore. The soccer ball and sketchpad were immediately tucked into the nest of roots as both children hopped down onto the sand.

"Where were you guys?" Jaxon and Allie asked at the same time. "We missed you today!"

"Oh, we were taking a long rest. Waking up out of the sand takes a great deal of work and we were all quite tired," Shalini replied. "Now, would you like to go for a ride?"

"Oh yes, very much!" said Allie. She remembered how much fun it had been to ride on the dragons' backs last year. "But the water is really cold," she added.

"Well, if you sit high on our backs you won't get wet," Shiran said, laughing. The dragon's laugh was a little bit like the ringing of cymbals, chiming and vibrating. It was a beautiful sound to Allie. It echoed against the cliffs and carried across the water so the sound lasted for a long moment. In a flash she was by Shalini's side, ready to climb aboard the beautiful creature.

Shiran and Shalini stretched their necks out long and low on the sand and rested their chins on the low rocks. Allie climbed onto Shalini's neck and slowly worked her way between the spikes and up onto the mother dragon's back. She settled herself among the shimmering magenta scales and took hold of the blue spike directly in front of her. Shalini's scales were smooth as glass, but the spikes were a bit rougher, easier to grip.

"I'm ready," she told Shalini.

Jaxon had scrambled onto Shiran's tall back and perched himself at the highest point. "Hey, Allie, I'm higher up than you are!" he called. He hung on to Shiran's shimmering blue back, both hands around the dragon's glowing pink spike. The late afternoon sun was lighting up Shiran's colors as Jaxon watched with delight. "I'm ready, too," he said.

Shoram and Shyla, having shaken the sleep dust out of their eyes and done a few dragon hops up and down the beach to wake up, were also ready. They crowded close to look up at the two children. They had never taken a human child fire-fishing before, and they were excited.

Shalini and Shiran waded slowly into the water, careful to keep their passengers high and dry. It was the children's first dragon ride since last summer, and the adult dragons didn't want to move too quickly. The two young dragons, on the other hand, dove right in, swimming circles around each other and splashing with their tails. Shoram was lightning fast in the water, his trumpeting announcing that they were all heading out to sea.

On the way the young dragons took to playing games. Shyla popped up right beside Allie's leg. "Oh my gosh," Allie exclaimed. "Where did you come from?" Shyla smiled shyly and Allie smiled back. At that Shyla dove and, with a quick flick of her tail, disappeared beneath the surface.

Meanwhile Shoram was following his father, gliding underwater where he couldn't be seen. When he saw his chance he came up next to Jaxon, trumpeting loudly.

"Whoa!" Jaxon cried. "You scared me! I almost fell off!" Shiran was about to scold his son, but as he turned his huge head, Jaxon reached out to touch the little green dragon's small, sharp horns. "You're awesome . . ."

Shalini swam up. "Are you children hungry?" she asked. Were they ever! Shoram insisted he was starving, and Jaxon agreed. It was dinnertime and the excitement of the ocean had made them all ravenous.

"Do you like salmon?" Shalini asked.

"Oh yes, we do!" chimed Jaxon. "We have grilled salmon all the time at Carla's Restaurant on the Coast."

"Mom fixes it for dinner sometimes, too," said Allie. *But dragon-caught salmon?* she wondered. *How would they cook it?*

Shiran called out to the young dragons who were swimming close beside the children. "Shoram, Shyla, would you like to bring us some salmon for dinner?"

"Yum! I'll get the first one, I bet!" Shoram trumpeted, and Shyla nodded happily. And off they swam, disappearing beneath the waves.

Since ancient times, the dragons of Shi Shi have fire-fished. Despite their size, their wit and agility make them very successful. The dragons swim a short distance off-shore until they find a school of salmon. The fish feel and see the hungry creatures coming, of course. A fully grown dragon is the size of a school bus, remember! The fish scatter. The dragon pursues a single fish, and when she gets close enough, opens her mouth and BLAST! she lets out a burst of fire. The fire-burst stuns and cooks the fish all at once. A dragon may eat his catch on the spot or carry it back to the beach for later. You can tell where a dragon is fire-fishing by the telltale little wisps of steam rising from the water's surface. These may look like fog and mist at first, but if you watch closely you'll see a pattern. First the steam lies low over the water, then it slowly climbs into a thin column. That tells you there's a dragon fire-fishing down below.

Jaxon pointed to a spot just a few yards away from where he and Allie were sitting, high above the surf. A sparkling green head was emerging from the choppy water. "Look Allie, Shoram's already caught a fish!"

While the young dragons continued fire-fishing, Shiran and Shalini swam back to the beach and gently let Jaxon and Allie down onto the sand.

Allie said, "Wasn't that great? It feels good to be on the ground again, though!" Jaxon nodded, his eyes still on the horizon. He was dreaming of another ride, Allie decided.

The afternoon turned toward evening. Shoram and his sister came out of the water, each one holding a cooked salmon in his mouth. The two dragons placed their catch on a flat rock and headed back for more.

"*Mmm,* delicious," Shiran said, as he munched his salmon, together with a big bite of popcorn seaweed. Shiran loved the combination of this seaweed, so easy to find floating in the surf, and fire-roasted salmon. When he munched on those puffy little balloons that made the seaweed float, they popped in his mouth with a delicious sea salt flavor.

"Here, try some," he said to Allie. She smiled a *thank you* and popped a bite in her mouth.

"It's salty and crunchy! Here Jaxon, try some," Allie said.

Now, the salmon was good to eat, but it was a whole fish with the eyeballs still in and scales on its body.

Allie looked at the eyeballs. They were kind of creepy. Neither she nor Jaxon much liked the taste of the skin. But once you peeled back the skin to get at the meat, the salmon tasted great. If only those eyeballs weren't there . . . Jaxon guessed what Allie was thinking. He picked out one of the eyeballs and threw it at her.

"Jaxon!" shrieked Allie, batting away the eyeball. Shoram trumpeted with delight. Shiran smiled. These human children were so much like his dragon offspring—one always tormenting the other.

Shyla saw what was going on. This was just the kind of thing her little green brother did to her. Once Shoram had tucked a sea slug inside her salmon and waited until she bit into it! Shyla hurried over and stood next to Allie. Aiming her gaze at Jaxon, she lowered her head, already quite large even though she was a young dragon.

"Oh, all right. I was just kidding around," said Jaxon as he threw away the second eyeball.

"Thanks, Shyla," whispered Allie.

Jaxon asked, "Do you think we could visit your caves sometime?"

Shalini smiled and puffed a gentle steam ring into the air. "It might be difficult to get to, and it can be quite slippery for human feet," she said. "But you'd find it beautiful inside, I think."

A dragon's cave is an amazing place. The Shi Shi dragons don't hoard gold and jewels the way Western dragons do. Their treasure is the sea life that lives on the walls of the caves and in the little tide pools that form when the tide goes out. If you entered the cave when the dragon wasn't at home, you would see barnacles lining the walls, making clicking-clacking noises as they opened and closed their shells. You would see different colored seaweeds stuck to the walls, too, protecting these tiny animals from drying out while forming a soft wall for the dragons to lean against. The pools are filled with beautiful sea life— anemones, sea stars, hermit crabs, periwinkle snails, maybe a small fish or two, and sometimes a bright orange sea cucumber tucked under the rocks. It's a different kind of treasure that the Shi Shi dragons protect.

The six friends ate salmon until they were all quite satis-fied. By now the sun had set and the moon was rising.

"Time for bed," Shalini sighed. The night grew brighter and brighter as the moon threw a long, rippling carpet of light across the water to the southwest. Shiran agreed, and together the dragon family began moving toward their caves.

Shoram said, "I'm not sleepy at all. I want to stay here with Jaxon."

"You don't want to feel that sharp tip on Mom's tail, do you?" his sister reminded him.

"Okay, okay, I'm coming," he said. And both Shoram and Shyla hopped and flapped toward their smaller caves.

Allie and Jaxon realized they were pretty tired, too. They climbed up on the weathered log and walked its length toward the beacon of their campfire. They could see their parents sitting near the fire, watching the moon rise.

As Jaxon and Allie approached, Mom and Dad thought they saw—were those *stars* in their children's eyes? They knew there was magic in the air around Shi Shi but, being wise parents, they didn't ask questions. Allie and Jaxon snuggled in close.

"Why do you two smell so fishy?" asked Mom. Jaxon just smiled. Before long the whole family crawled into their sleeping bags for the night. As the fire died down, Jaxon and Allie went to sleep dreaming of their dragon friends.

three THE GREAT DRAGON CASTLE

One sunny day Jaxon and Allie decided to see if they could spend the entire afternoon with the dragons. Most of their visits had been at dusk, and Allie was particularly curious about how the sunshine would make those dramatic dragon scales glitter and change color. So after lunch the two took off down to Point of the Arches, Allie with her colored pencils and sketchbook, and Jaxon with his soccer ball and favorite soccer cap. In no time they found the magic log and tiptoed easily down to their favorite spot at the big end. By now the dragons knew this to be the children's waiting place.

As soon as Allie and Jaxon got settled and looked toward the ocean, they realized all four dragons were lying around on the beach to the south, soaking up the sun. Before they could call to the dragon family, Jaxon suddenly pointed to a place at the far end of the beach.

"Hey, those rocks . . . down there! I just saw something moving . . ." Just then a large cloud passed in front of the sun. Allie shivered.

The two of them stared hard into the distance. Sure enough, as Allie watched, she began to make out a dull gray-green shape moving slowly back and forth on the beach. Then Jaxon saw another hint of movement, very slight. It was hard to be sure what they were seeing. The moving shapes looked so much like the rocks, a mossy greenish gray. Finally Allie pointed out a third much smaller shape, which hopped about now and then.

Allie and Jaxon watched a few minutes longer. Finally the two of them hopped down off the log and walked over to Shyla and Shoram.

"You guys see those shapes?" Jaxon pointed. "Are those dragons hanging around over there?"

Allie whispered to Shyla, "Your mom and dad warned us about some mean dragons that live a couple of beaches over." Shyla turned to look.

"Yep, that's the Zorg family. I must tell Dad you've seen them, Allie," she said. "I don't like being around Zorg—he's scary. But Zonta—that's his son—well, sometimes he's okay, when he's in a playing mood." The dragons and children watched for a few minutes more, but the gray-green dragons didn't come any closer.

Jaxon turned to Shoram. "Well, anyway, we came down here to see if you all wanted to build a giant sand castle. You'd be great at it!"

Shoram and Shyla exchanged knowing glances. Shoram flashed his sister a toothy grin, and she rolled her eyes.

"Sure," said Shyla, "we know how to move the sand around. But what's a *castle*?" Castles weren't part of their dragon history.

Shoram interrupted. "What's that black and white thing under your arm, Jaxon? Do you use it to build sand castles?"

"No, silly, that's my soccer ball." Jaxon's eyes lit up. "Hey, I could teach you guys to play soccer!"

Allie said, "No soccer today, Jaxon. You promised we'd build a sand castle, remember?"

Jaxon sighed, but put his soccer ball in its safe nook among the roots of the tree. He and Allie took turns explaining to the dragons about real castles. Then the children set about building a huge battlement in the smooth sand. Allie and Jaxon dug with their hands and their beach shovels. The sand was damp and packed easily into the lines and walls they were building. Shyla and Shoram watched the children for a few minutes until they saw the plan taking shape. Then the two young dragons dug with their front feet and pushed piles of sand around with their tails.

This is sure to be the biggest sand castle anyone's ever built, thought Jaxon. The outer walls were 12 feet square and 3 feet high. If the children had lain down on the damp sand inside it, they would have been completely hidden from an outsider's view.

They were beginning to dig the big moat around the outer walls, when Allie looked up and gasped. "Jaxon, look!" she said.

Just at the edge of the cliff a small gray-green dragon was moving closer to their growing castle, taking tiny steps as if he was hoping no one would notice him. This new dragon had none of the luster or brilliant colors that the Shi Shi dragons had. He moved slowly and heavily, and Allie wondered if he was a very good swimmer. The dragon's head swung back and forth, low to the ground, as if he were sniffing for answers to something he didn't understand.

"He doesn't look scary," said Jaxon, but just the same he got up and walked over to stand beside Shoram. Lowering his head slightly, Shoram growled, and the strange dragon stopped in his tracks. Shyla glared at her brother. "Hey Zonta," she said, "want to work on this sand castle with us?"

Zonta looked wistfully at the castle. Then he looked at the two human children. But he didn't move. Allie realized that this young dragon was afraid of them. *Jaxon's right,* she thought. *He's not so scary.*

"Come on," she said. "I'm Allie and this is my brother Jaxon." She waited for a minute. Zonta didn't move a single scale or spike. He seemed frozen in place. "You could help us dig out the moat, see, over here . . ." Allie motioned toward the outer edge of the wall they had built. "Then we can surround the castle with sea water. It'll be cool!"

Shoram, too, began encouraging the reluctant dragon, and pretty soon they were all digging out the big moat. Zonta wasn't very careful with his digging and sand was flying everywhere. "Hey, watch it there!" said Jaxon. "You're getting sand in my eyes."

Zonta stopped what he was doing. "Sorry," he said. He pouted for a minute, not liking to be scolded. But when he went back to building, he tried to be more careful. With so many hands and feet and tails working together, the moat was soon finished. Jaxon spotted a board among the piles of driftwood.

"The perfect drawbridge!" he cried, as he began working it into the sand around the entrance.

Then the group set to work on the inside of the castle. They built up the center part so it had some rooms and a couple of interior towers. As she scooped and built, Allie imagined she was an eagle looking down from a great height at the outlines of the rooms. Shoram went off to find some logs and rocks to fortify the towers. When he came rolling them back, Zonta frowned at them.

"Those will never work," he grumped. "What do you want to do with those dumb logs, anyway?"

Shoram said, "They'll strengthen the corner towers. C'mon, it's worth a try." Still frowning, Zonta helped Shoram roll one of the big logs up against the base of the tower. With their front legs, the two stood the log upright. Then they wiggled the base of the log into the sand, digging it in deep so it would stand up by itself. Both young dragons were so intent on their work that they hardly noticed how well they were getting along.

"This is fun!" Zonta said at last. "Let's take that big rock and put it inside the castle for the base of one of the inside towers." With a great deal of pushing and shoving, the group moved the rock across the drawbridge and into the castle. They all agreed it made a grand cornerstone for the interior walls and tower.

"Let's start decorating, Shyla," called Allie. She collected strands of kelp and draped them across Shyla's purple back to carry to the castle. There they placed kelp streamers at the tops of the towers, so they would flutter in the breeze like flags.

Shyla especially loved scallop shells, several of which she kept in her little cave. Pointing out a pile of them she said to Allie, "Let's line these up along the top of the front wall."

"Great idea!" said Allie, placing the shells. "Look at the pattern they make," she said. "Their shadows on the sand look like ripples in the water."

Jaxon, Zonta, and Shoram went off to find colored sea-weed and interesting rocks to decorate the other walls.

They found some of the shimmering dark red seaweed to put over the entrance.

"I know!" said Zonta. "Let's get those purple and orange sea stars. They'll look great on the inside walls."

"No!" replied Shoram and Jaxon forcefully. "We'd have to pull them off their rocks, and that'd tear lots of their tube feet. That might kill them."

"So? Who cares?" retorted Zonta.

"We do!" Jaxon shot back, looking him directly in the eye. Zonta looked away and stared down at the sand. "Well . . . we could take some of the hermit crabs out of the big tide pool and put them in the moat. They'd be okay in the water, right? When we're done with our castle we could put them back in the pool."

The three of them agreed. They began trying to catch some of the bigger hermit crabs. Zonta and Shoram were hopeless at the task. Their claws were too big, and they stumbled and tumbled around in the rocks as the crabs scuttled out of their way. But Jaxon was quick and fast, and he soon caught seven crabs of different sizes. Carefully, he carried them over to the moat and put them in the water. Zonta lumbered along after him, and Shoram skipped ahead.

Allie and Shyla had been looking for shells to decorate more of the castle. Once when Allie glanced over at the big rocks, she saw Zorgina watching. The big dragon's head drooped, and Allie was sad for a moment. "Do you think she'd like to help?" she asked. Shyla nodded. "Want to help us decorate?" she called out. But Zorgina solemnly shook her head no and continued to watch.

At that point Zorg moved in closer. All of them stopped what they were doing, even Zonta. Allie shivered as she remembered Shiran's warning. Zorg ignored them all, though, and stomped around on the sand a short distance away. He was close to Shiran in size, but rather scrawny. Zorg wasn't as sleek as the large blue dragon, either. There were scratches on some of his scales, and in a few places the scales were missing entirely so that only Zorg's thick

grayish hide showed. But his claws were long and hard, and his wings revealed powerful flying muscles.

"Why is he scowling at us like that?" Allie asked Shoram.

The green dragon shrugged. "He's always thinking up some new kind of trouble," he said.

Zorg was careful not to approach Shalini, who was watching the sand castle construction with great delight. But he soon spied something that tempted him. A moment later, Zorg had Jaxon's soccer ball between the claws of his heavy front feet.

"Jaxon, look!" cried Allie. Jaxon dropped the shells he was holding and started in the direction of his precious soccer ball. Lucky for him, though, Shiran had given up his snooze in the sun and had been eyeing the dull green dragon with a steady glare. Shiran stepped firmly in front of Jaxon and hissed quietly, "Leave him to me, young man." Jaxon stopped in his tracks, but he was no longer interested in the sand castle. Zorg stomped around, tossing the ball in the air. Now and then he roared at the seagulls as they flew overhead. Zorg must have been watching Jaxon practice headers, because he tried several of them. Then the ball hit one of his horns, and it collapsed with a sudden *whoosh!*

"No!" yelled Jaxon. "Your lousy horn ruined my favorite ball! You stupid dragon! Get lost!"

Zorg looked up. He blew a blast of steam in Jaxon's direction and growled, "Too bad it wasn't your head, you pesky little human." By this time Shalini had aligned herself beside Shiran, protecting the children and the sand castle. Zorg turned away, leaving the flattened ball on the beach as he shambled off to the rocks where Zorgina sat in the sand.

"He's horrible!" Jaxon stormed about. "Now how am I going to get my ball fixed?" He kicked hard at the ground and a spray of sand went flying. Shyla and Shoram watched him in silence. Zonta glanced over at the castle.

"Dad can help you fix it when we get home, Jaxon," Allie tried to comfort her brother. "Listen, you've got to stay away from Zorg like Shiran said, okay?"

After a while they convinced Jaxon to go back to decorating the sand castle. Soon the castle walls shone with shells, sand-polished stones of red and brown, and patterns made out of driftwood. Kelp ribbons flickered from the tops of the towers. The children and dragons stepped back to admire their work.

"Hey, these two towers are shorter than the others," said Allie. "We need a taller tower right over here," she said, pointing to one corner of the castle wall.

Shyla rubbed her nose with the tip of her tail, flicked her ears, and said, "You're right. I know—I'll just lie down alongside the wall and point my tail up there. That would make it the tallest tower in the whole castle!"

With that, Shyla lay down along one side of the battlement and stuck her tail straight up at the corner. It reached six feet into the air! Then Shyla dipped her tail down low for a moment so Allie could drape it with a few kelp streamers.

Shyla pointed her tail straight out once more, and gave it a graceful wave. The streamers fluttered just right! But in a few minutes Shyla got tired of being a wall support and started to feel wiggly. She tried hard to make her tail a tall, straight tower, but her wiggly feeling kept making it tip and wobble.

Jaxon and Allie laughed. "That's okay, Shyla. Better take a break!"

Not to be outdone, Shoram lay down along the opposite wall and stuck his tail straight up at the corner to contribute his own tower. Jaxon placed kelp streamers on the tip of Shoram's tail, and they waved nicely in the breeze. But despite the younger dragon's desire to show up his sister, he, too, wiggled and wobbled. Being a wall support was harder than it looked.

Now Zonta wanted in on the action. He crawled into the interior of the castle and put his tail up along one of the inside towers. Allie and Jaxon draped strings of kelp across his tail, too, and watched the streamers as they fluttered.

"Wow," said Jaxon, "this castle looks amazing!"

"Hey, look at Shoram's red-orange spikes," said Allie. "They make that wall look like it's on fire!"

"Yeah, the sun on Shyla's spikes is doing the same thing. Way cool. . . .You could draw a great picture of this when we get back to camp, Sis," he said.

The two were so absorbed in their castle that they didn't notice a young deer coming out of the forest. Her brown fur made her almost invisible against the driftwood, and she knew how to step silently in the sand. But Zorg saw the doe. Still angry that Shiran had forced him to retreat, he roared a long stream of fire at the doe, then snatched at her. She leaped, bounding back to the safety of the trees.

"*Harrrumpf,*" growled Zorg as he stomped off in the other direction.

Shoram, Shyla, and Zonta had been trying to keep their tails up straight, while at the same time turning their heads to see what was going on. At last Shoram had had enough. He wanted to see the whole castle!

Shoram stuck his head up over the edge of the wall and trumpeted, "Pretty nice, isn't it?" Zonta saw Shoram's head and decided to have a look, too. He raised up, eye to eye with Shoram. Shoram ducked down. They ducked heads, playing can't-see-me until Shyla said, "Stop! You'll knock down the castle!"

Just then they noticed the tide coming in again. Shoram, Shyla, and Zonta stood in place until the water lapped at their bellies.

"It tickles," Shyla giggled. And as she giggled, she wiggled. And a wiggling dragon causes the sand to move. The wall next to Shyla began to crack and crumble. The water tickled Shoram's and Zonta's bellies, as well. Pretty soon none of them could keep still. The castle was one big mass of giggling, wiggling dragons covered in cracking, crumbling sand. Jaxon and Allie laughed hysterically at the sight.

Finally Shyla and Shoram, followed by Zonta, got up and moved as the waves came in more and more strongly, washing away the castle walls. A few more waves, and the castle was only a large mound of sand scattered with a few pebbles and strings of kelp. But before the castle moat had flooded completely, Jaxon remembered the hermit crabs. He ran to collect them and return them to their tide pool. As he put the creatures back in the briny water, he was almost sure he heard them say *thank you. But no,* he thought, *that couldn't be. Or could it?*

Jaxon and Allie were so intent on the waves demolishing their sand castle that they didn't notice how Shiran kept moving to position himself between the children and Zorg. Both the adult dragons kept a careful watch as the sand castle dissolved into the beach.

It was getting close to dinnertime. Shyla said to Zonta, "I'm hungry. Want to go fishing with us?"

Zonta shuffled his hind feet in the sand a moment. "Yeah, sure," he said. "I'm hungry, too." Zonta didn't want to show it, but secretly he was glad to be invited. He'd never learned how to fish very well; for some reason his father had refused to teach him. All three young dragons now hopped and flapped their way into the deeper water off-shore, and soon disappeared beneath the surf.

"I'm kinda glad they didn't offer us any this time," said Allie. "I'm ready for Mom's food."

When the two of them arrived back at camp, Allie said excitedly to her mother, "Did you see the great castle we made?"

Mom looked quizzical. "What castle?" she said.

"The one down there that's washing away in the waves!" Jaxon was sure the castle had been big enough to be seen from camp.

But when Allie turned and looked down the beach, she couldn't see any part of the castle, not even the big lump of sand or the scatterings of rocks. Then she remembered: they had crossed out of the dragons' land back into the human realm. "I wish you'd seen it, Mom," she said, disappointed. "It was the biggest castle we've ever built, and it had a huge moat . . . "

Mom gave her daughter a big hug. "That's the way of sand castles, honey. They can't last forever. But their magic will stay in your mind and heart." She poured Allie and Jaxon each a cup of lemonade. "And you can go back there any time you want, in your memory."

Dad was now holding what was left of Jaxon's soccer ball. He said, "You know, Allie, I'll bet you could draw us a very accurate picture of that castle." He handed the flattened ball back to his son. "Don't worry about this, buddy. We'll fix it as soon as we get home." In no time, both children were chattering to their parents about all the details of the castle. But they didn't mention the dragons. How could they explain such magical creatures?

four AN EERIE LIGHT

Several weeks went by. Back home in Seattle, Jaxon and Allie longed to be back at the beach with the dragons, and they continually imagined what Shoram and Shyla were doing each day. But their parents had to work. *No telling when we'll be able to go back,* thought Allie.

Jaxon rode his bike to the library almost daily, looking up details of dragon history and lore. He found one book about Asian dragons that lived in the water. The pictures didn't look quite like the Shi Shi dragons, but the book still held plenty of information for Jaxon to ponder.

Allie spent hours trying to capture what the dragons looked like with her sumi-e brushes and ink. She especially wanted to paint their afternoon making a sand castle with the dragons. Her mom had helped her some with the brushwork, teaching her how to hold the brush and make it dance across the page.

"When are we going back to Shi Shi?" she kept asking. "I really miss being there."

"How about next week?" Mom replied. "Your dad has to work, but I know how much you kids like to be out on the beach. The three of us can go . . . if you and your brother are willing to help carry more of the food."

Allie smiled. "Sure thing!"

"You bet!" said Jaxon. Sister and brother high-fived.

The two of them jumped into preparations for the beach trip. "I'll leave my soccer ball behind this time," said Jaxon, "so there's more room for dinner." He almost blurted out that they could eat dragon-caught salmon for dinner, but caught himself just in time. *But I'll need to take the library book about dragons,* he thought.

A few days later they were back on the beach. Their old campsite was still intact and they only needed to secure the tarps. Then they moved right back into the shelter and built a new fire in the fire ring.

After dinner the youngsters raced down to Point of the Arches and the magic log. They couldn't wait to meet the dragons again. It was getting dark, but after some pleading and cajoling, their mother allowed them to go. She recalled her own childhood adventures on the beach at dusk, and she wanted her children to have their own fond memories to look back on one day.

As Jaxon and Allie sat on the magic log, they noticed a sudden glow of light coming from a nearby cave around the point. It started as a soft white glimmer, and as they watched it pulsed brighter and brighter. Gradually the light faded and went out.

"What was that?" Allie exclaimed.

"I don't know," said Jaxon, still peering at the place where the light had been. "Let's go find out!"

Just then they spotted Shoram and Shyla on the beach. In seconds Jaxon and Allie had jumped off the log and were standing beside the young dragons.

"Did you see that?" said Allie.

"It was over there," said Jaxon, pointing. Shoram and Shyla looked.

"Uh-oh," said Shoram. He sounded serious. "I think Zorg may be up to one of his phosphorescent tricks again . . ."

"Well, let's go see!" said Jaxon.

"You shall not do that, young sir," Shiran announced. Jaxon hadn't even noticed his arrival. How could such a huge dragon be so quiet? "You must keep your distance from Zorg."

Just then the light burst forth from the darkness again. A roaring sound and then another burst of bluish light began to glow from Zorg's cave. Now Shoram and Shyla wanted to go and see what was happening, too. Shoram said to his father, "Shyla and I can protect Jaxon and Allie. We'll take them out to that big rock just offshore. That way we can look straight into the cave and Zorg won't even see us. Please, Dad, Mom?"

Shalini didn't like any part of this. "No," she said firmly.

"Let me tell you Zorg's story, as I heard it told many years ago. Then maybe you'll understand our caution. Zorg was a handsome young dragon with beautiful, shimmering green scales. He and Zorgina lived in the sea together. Zonta had just hatched, and that little fellow was a wonderful silvery blue. They knew how to fish for salmon as we do. But other great beasts live under the water as well, and some have magical powers." Jaxon and Allie forgot for a moment about the lights in the cave as they listened to Shalini's voice.

"One day the worst of these enemies came to take over Zorg's sea territory. He tried to fight them but he was no match for their devious powers. Zorg was badly beaten. He didn't really have a chance. Even with Zorgina's help, he was only one dragon against these monsters." Jaxon was now seated on a large, flat rock, picturing a ferocious fight that churned up the seas like a typhoon.

Shalini continued. "They drove Zorg out of his home and up onto the beach. After that he lost his confidence and took up being a bully. He began to enjoy being mean to others, just as his opponents had been mean to him. In a mere 25 years, Zorg's scales had turned to the dull gray-green that they are now." Allie glanced at the cave as it flashed light and then went dark again.

"That was many years ago, but nothing seems to have changed for Zorg. And dragons who enjoy hurting others are highly unpredictable. They can be dangerous, even to other dragons. Now do you understand why we don't want you to go near him?" asked Shalini.

Jaxon had heard of Asian dragons that lived in kingdoms beneath the sea. Could Zorg be one of those? He'd read about some of their underwater battles, too. He knew that most of the defeated dragons died, rarely escaping the wrath of the invading enemies. Zorg was probably lucky to be alive. Jaxon had to admit it was probably a good idea to stay out of that angry dragon's way.

But what was causing the strange light show? Just then

they heard a loud roar. And again, a flash of light from the cave.

"Mom, Dad, could you come with us so we can show Jaxon and Allie?" Shyla asked. The adult dragons agreed. *Sure, if they all went out to the rock it would be safe,* thought Shalini. *After all, Zorg was only one grumpy dragon and they were four dragons and two humans.*

Jaxon and Allie climbed aboard the blue and magenta dragons. Together with Shoram and Shyla, they swam out a short distance, leaving a glowing phosphorescence in their wake. Soon the group had arrived near a cluster of large, flat rocks just opposite the mysterious cave.

As they settled themselves on the rocks, Zorg emerged and began heading out into the breaking waves. Shiran and Shalini stiffened and quietly moved their wings to shield the children from view. What Zorg did next amazed them all. They watched as the gray-green dragon took in mouthful after mouthful of the phosphorescent water, straining it between his teeth. Then he lumbered back to his cave as though carrying something in his mouth. Zorg began dropping lumps of colorless plankton and jellyfish on a bed of kelp in the center of the cave. Jaxon and Allie looked quizzically at Shoram and Shyla. Was Zorg going to eat all these sea creatures? Why was he piling them up?

"Keep watching," said Shoram.

Then Zorg pointed his nose straight up toward the ceiling of the cave, took a deep breath, and let out a roar. A blast of fire shot upward, and the entire cave lit up. As the light died down, Jaxon and Allie and the young dragons saw the mound of kelp beginning to glow just a little. It got brighter and brighter until a cool white light filled the whole cave, spilling into the darkness beyond.

"Wow," whispered Jaxon. The light seemed to pulsate in waves. After some time the glow began to fade. Zorg let out another blast of fire and the process started all over again.

The gray-green dragon's face had lost its usual scowl. He seemed pleased with his creation of light. *Maybe doing this cheers him up,* Allie thought. The group could see Zorgina and Zonta watching from the shadows. They clearly enjoyed his light show, as well. Zonta hopped a little each time his father gave out a good, loud blast and made the cave glow.

After a while the mound stopped glowing. Jaxon and Allie heard a low rumble as Zorgina and her dragon son spoke to the huge dragon. Soon Zorg returned to the water, collected more phosphorescent animals, and constructed a fresh mound. He created yet another light show for his family. But these sea creatures grew tired and stopped glowing as brightly. Zorg was tired, too. He left the jellyfish in a heap on the floor and motioned to Zorgina and Zonta. The three of them slowly made their way toward the back of the cave for the night.

Jaxon whispered to Shiran, "He shouldn't do that! Those jellyfish and plankton need to go back in the water. The special effects were great and everything, but he shouldn't just leave them on the floor to die."

Shiran nodded in sad agreement. "That's just the way Zorg is."

Shalini turned to Jaxon and Allie. "It's late, friends. Time to go home." In a flash the Shi Shi dragons had transported them back to the beach, safe and dry. Jaxon and Allie hurried back to camp. They weren't sure how long they had been gone, and hoped Mom wasn't worried. But they quickly discovered a strange thing about the difference between dragon time and human time. Allie and her brother had been gone only a few minutes! They were back in plenty of time for s'mores around the campfire before snuggling into their sleeping bags.

"You know, Jaxon," Allie said sleepily, "that light in Zorg's cave glowed just like the stars Mom and I glued on my bedroom ceiling at home. They glow after I turn out the lights at night."

"Only this was a whole lot brighter!" smiled Jaxon. And the two of them drifted off to sleep.

five AERIAL BATTLE

The next day began bright and sunny. Allie and Jaxon, wishing for another big adventure, were eager to get back to the dragons. So, after a big breakfast of eggs and toast seasoned with campfire smoke, they headed for the point.

No sooner had they climbed onto the magic log when they saw Shoram and Shyla coming out of their caves. The dragon brother and sister opened their mouths wide (boy, did those two have a lot of teeth!) as they stretched their wings to gather the sun's warmth. The children overheard young Shoram say, "The tide's way out today. Let's go explore the caves in the arches."

"I don't know . . ." said Shyla. She walked in a lazy circle, drawing in the sand with her tail.

"Hey, can we come along?" called Jaxon. Shyla looked up and brightened.

"Sure," Shoram answered.

His purple sister nodded, "Yes, we'll take you!"

Allie and Jaxon carefully climbed onto the backs of the young dragons. Allie wrapped her fingers firmly around one of Shyla's yellow-gold spikes. She looked at it closely. She wanted to remember every detail for her paintings.

Off they went, and soon the friends were exploring the fresh tide pools. The shaded pools were rich with sea life. "Hey, Shoram, look at these huge orange sea stars!" said Jaxon. Shyla flicked her tail gently across the water, watching as the anemones shuttered closed, then gracefully opened again.

The children studied the ceilings of the caves. The craggy surfaces, dripping with seaweed, were covered with barnacles, tiny snails, and mussels. The air was damp with sea spray. Allie said to Jaxon, "Do you think Zorg's underwater home was like this? It's so beautiful . . ."

No one paid attention to the sun moving higher in the sky. But after a while Shoram felt his stomach growling.

"I'm hungry," he said. "Let's go catch some fish."

"Good idea," Shyla replied. "But what about Jaxon and Allie? Is it all right to take them underwater?"

Just then Jaxon remembered something he had read in his library book. Dragons that lived under the sea were supposed to have special ways of breathing that let them live underwater as well as on land. *Could the dragons use their abilities to help humans stay underwater longer?* he wondered.

Shoram guessed what Jaxon was thinking. "I have an idea," he said. "We'll make a big air bubble around you just before we dive. That way you can breathe underwater! Okay?"

That sounded exciting! So with Allie and Jaxon high on their backs, the dragons headed out to sea. And sure enough, just before they were ready to dive, each dragon turned its head and blew a big protective air bubble around each child. Allie loved the way it felt inside her bubble, like a cocoon of soft air surrounding her. Jaxon thought of his bubble as a protective shield.

Shyla said, "All right now, remember: when you're running low on air, just pull!" The children had been instructed to keep hold of a spike as their dragon hosts swam underwater. They were to give three tugs whenever they needed to come up for air, so their dragon would know to head back to the water's surface.

Once the group was underwater, the fire-fishing began in earnest. Jaxon and Allie held tight to each dragon's back. They saw the fish scatter. Allie held her breath as each dragon pursued a fish and then let out a little blast of fire, steaming it to perfection. Allie was glad she'd had breakfast and wasn't hungry for whole steamed salmon, complete with skin and eyeballs. The dragons fished for a long time.

Suddenly Allie could sense her air running out. She tugged on Shyla's yellow-gold spike three times, and right away her dragon headed for the surface.

Shyla looked around at Allie. "You all right?"

"Yes!" said Allie. "You're really good at fire-fishing!"

"Thanks," said Shyla, and Allie thought she saw the dragon's color changing just slightly.

Shoram and Jaxon popped up close by. "That was fun!" Jaxon hollered. Allie nodded and waved.

Just then Shalini and Shiran appeared in the water beside the youngsters. "Perhaps now we should all catch some more fish and take them back to the beach for an afternoon snack with seaweed popcorn," said Shiran. His voice sounded stern but his eyes were twinkling. The two young dragons headed back to the water and soon there were enough fish in a shady tide pool for a wonderful meal later.

Over on Stinky Fish Beach, Zorg, Zorgina, and Zonta were sitting on the rocks. As usual, Zorgina looked quite sad. "Zorg," she said finally, "we're hungry. We haven't had any fresh fish for three days. The fish we have is starting to stink!"

Zorg's stomach was rumbling. It wasn't a gentle rumbling, either. It was *loud*. Like rocks tumbling around in a metal furnace.

"Well, I guess I'd better do something," he said. "Hey, I know! The Shi Shi dragons just went fishing—you heard them splashing and chattering. They had those silly human children with them. I'll bet they've got their catch in a tide pool over there." *Why should they get all the best salmon?* he grumbled to himself. Zorg belted out a gravelly laugh. "Ashy-headed human lovers! When I get through with their little tidey-pool they'll have Fish Surprise. . . . And the surprise will be—no fish!"

"But . . ." Zorgina began.

Zorg cackled, ignoring her. He'd show those prissy Shi Shi dragons. He stretched his leathery wings, swished his tail back and forth, and crouched low. With a mighty leap, he vaulted into the air and spread his wings wide. Zorg slowly spiraled upward, gaining altitude as he headed off around the point toward Shi Shi beach. Zonta watched as his father got smaller and smaller, until he was just a dark dot in the sky.

Back at Shi Shi the cheerful dragons and their human friends were relaxing on the sand, soaking up sunshine after their swim. Shiran let out a big yawn. Then he saw a strange dot in the sky, growing steadily larger.

Uh-oh, Shiran thought, *guess that nap will have to wait.* This wouldn't be the first time Zorg had stolen their catch after a successful round of fire-fishing.

Shiran quickly alerted the others. "We have an unwelcome visitor," he said, gesturing toward the shape in the sky. "It's Zorg. I think he's after our fish."

"Oh dear me," said Shalini as she glanced over at the children.

"He won't get our fish if I have anything to say about it!" roared Shiran. But he also knew that Zorg was quick and skilled at stealing. He would have to be agile and clever to fend off the gray-green dragon.

Shalini spoke firmly to the human children. "You mustn't get in the middle of a dragon fight. Now quickly . . . over there behind your log. Stay down low and out of the way."

Jaxon took his sister's hand and the two ran behind the magic log. They crouched behind the big roots where they could peek around and see what was happening.

Zorg landed on the beach with a roar and a burst of fire. "I demand fish!" he snarled at Shiran and Shalini. The young dragons were hunched down close together by the pool that held the fish.

"This catch is ours!" roared Shiran, as he stepped directly in front of Zorg.

"Give them to me, or I'll take them!"

Zorg blew a great blast of fire into the sky, and Jaxon and Allie felt the sudden heat on their faces.

Shiran and Shalini both charged Zorg at the same time, heads down and wings back, forcing him to step backward. Shyla whispered under her breath, "Go, Mom and Dad!"

Zorg was lazy and disagreeable, but he was also intelligent. The bully dragon had already guessed that the fish were stored in the pool that Shoram and Shyla were guarding. Zorg calculated that if he took to the air and pretended to fly away, he could turn back quickly, make a swooping dive, and grab the fish in the pool as he flew by. Zorg turned and opened out his wings as if he were about to take off.

But Shiran, too, was wise and experienced. The great blue dragon had weathered many encounters with dragons like Zorg. As he watched the dull green dragon retreat into the air, he leaped into flight. Shalini followed his lead. Together they pursued the fish thief, arcing and twisting in step with Zorg's every move. Suddenly, though, the gray-green dragon made an abrupt turn and swooped down toward the tide pool.

Zorg turned toward Shiran. "Those fish are mine!" he snarled. Shiran let out a blast of fire. Zorg twisted upward so that the fire just missed him. Shalini flew above, ready to force the thief to the ground, when Zorg twisted again and slipped between them, heading once more for the pool.

Shyla saw him coming. "Shoram!" she screamed. "Get behind those rocks! Zorg could burn us!" Allie and Jaxon held tightly to one another. They knew they were safe, but their friends were in great danger. Now Jaxon understood

Shiran's warning. Zorg was not someone to fool with when he was angry. And it seemed he was always angry.

Shoram and Shyla jumped behind the tall rocks nearby, and Zorg saw his chance. He swooped down low and, opening his mouth wide, snatched up a clump of fish and seaweed as he flew over the pool. Shiran was not far behind. He managed to bump Zorg off course as he was lifting away. "Get out of here!" Zorg roared with a fiery blast. Jaxon caught a whiff of scorched dragon scales.

Shalini followed the gray-green dragon as he gained altitude. "And don't come back!" she roared, blowing her own blast of fire.

As soon as Zorg was out of sight, the young humans and dragons cautiously walked back out onto the open beach. Shiran and Shalini, both breathing hard, landed beside the pool. One glance told them that Zorg had taken at least half their catch. "There are still a few left, anyway," Shalini sighed. She sniffed carefully around her children's faces and ears for any signs of singed scales, and said, "Thank goodness neither of you were hurt. Zorg's never come that close before."

"You guys are so brave!" said Allie. For a long moment she stood in the shadow of the great blue dragon, his head so far above hers in the sky.

"What a fight!" added Jaxon. "You guys were moving so fast! I couldn't keep up with all the twists and moves." Nothing in Jaxon's book on dragons had described anything so grand as what he had just witnessed.

The battle had made them all hungry. As the group enjoyed what was left of their snack, Shiran grew thoughtful. "You know," he said, "I think this is the beginning of a new phase for Zorg. I'm guessing he'll be back more often now to steal fish. Maybe next time we'll just fill the pool with rockfish instead of salmon. Then Zorg will be spitting bones all the way home!"

Shoram added, "Let's think up a whole bunch of ways that we can trick Zorg. This is going to be fun!"

"Nothing too scary, I hope," whispered Shyla. The purple dragon had stayed close to her mother ever since Zorg had disappeared in the sky.

six NOSY, NOISY NIJI

"I think I want to stay in camp for a while," said Allie the next morning. "I'm going to do a drawing of a battle between two dragons."

"Okay with me," Jaxon answered. "I need to look up some things in my book, anyway."

"I've never seen you two so interested in the same subject before," Mom said. "What's got you so interested in dragons all of a sudden?"

"Oh, nothing," both children said together.

Their mother smiled and said, "You know, kids, I used to come here when I was about your age. I thought more than once that the tall rocks moved, down there at Point of the Arches. Have you ever thought you saw something like that?"

Allie didn't say anything. She glanced at her brother. "Uh, yeah, maybe . . ." said Jaxon. Then he quickly looked down at his book. Did Mom know about *their* dragons?

As the morning wore on and the sun climbed higher, it got very warm on the beach. Shoram and Shyla decided to fly to the top of one of the outermost rock formations. It was a sea stack with a small group of fir trees on it, their branches twisted by the constant wind. It was that cool wind the young dragons were seeking. It was also a good place to keep an eye out for Zorg. The dragons called it Lookout Rock.

As soon as they were situated on their lookout, they spotted something. An eagle was circling overhead, scanning for food. As they watched, the great bird dove and grabbed a small seagull in its powerful talons, flew to a nearby tree, and perched to eat. Shoram marveled at the eagle's sharp eyesight.

After a little squirming and pushing, both dragons found good places to lie down in the shade of the firs. Shoram kept an eye on the horizon, half hoping Zorg might show up. He'd loved watching his father's powerful acrobatic flight the day before.

The two dragons hadn't been on Lookout Rock for long when Shyla heard a strange sound. Puzzled, she turned her head and looked around. *Cra-ack.* She heard it again. It sounded like a shell cracking. Shoram heard it, too.

"What do you suppose it is?" he said, trumpeting for emphasis.

"*Shhh!* Let's listen," Shyla whispered.

The young dragons looked here and there, craning their long necks in all directions to peer behind the trees and under the bushes that covered the rock. Shoram wished he had the eagle's keen vision just now.

Craack, craaack they heard again.

Suddenly Shyla noticed something funny about a patch of soft green moss. It was moving! With each cracking sound, the moss moved a little bit. Then all at once the moss was pushed aside, and they saw . . . a small dragon slowly emerging from an egg! He was a tiny fellow only about six inches long, much smaller than either Shoram or Shyla had been when they hatched. And he was multi-colored. The tiny dragon let out a high-pitched squeak.

"Who are you?" asked Shoram.

"*Squeak, squeak, sq squeak,*" the little dragon answered.

"You look like a rainbow!" said Shyla. "How did you get here?"

The little dragon turned and looked at the egg. "*Squeak, squeak,*" he answered, as if to say, *I came from that egg, silly.*

"No, no—that's not what we meant. Where's your mother who laid the egg?" Shoram and Shyla knew very well that under normal conditions, dragon mothers stayed with their eggs until they hatched. But this little fellow was all alone, hatching by himself. *Very strange,* thought Shoram.

The little dragon shrugged. His wings were still wet and stuck to his sides.

"Well then, we'll just have to give you a name," Shyla announced.

"*Squeak, squeak, squeak-a-squeak,*" said the hatchling, hopping about and stretching out his wings so they could dry in the warm sun.

"I know," said Shyla, "we'll call you Rainbow Sky."

"No! He's more than just a rainbow. He's a mystery dragon," said Shoram. "We should call him something mysterious." He began thinking. Just then the wind picked up, and it whistled through the leaves. *Niji, niji, niji,* the wind seemed to say. Shoram liked the sound. "How about Niji?" he asked.

The little dragon jumped up and down, squeaking excitedly.

"Looks like that's a winner," said Shyla. "This is getting to be one exciting summer!"

"Sure is!" Shoram agreed.

Shoram gently lifted Niji out onto a sunnier part of the rock where the hatchling could stay warm while his wings dried out. The brother and sister kept a sharp eye out for hungry eagles who might see the little dragon as a tasty bit of lunch. In a little while Niji's wings were dry, and he was hopping about and flapping his wings, eager to fly.

"Wait, wait," said Shoram. "There are strong winds here. How about if you hop on my back and we'll fly back to Shi Shi that way? Then you can meet our mom and dad . . . and Jaxon and Allie, if they're around. And you can practice flying out on the beach where it's not so windy."

"*Squeak, squeak,*" said Niji, as he hopped onto Shoram's neck. Soon the little hatchling was settled on the broad green back just between the dragon's wings.

Off they flew to Shi Shi. As they landed on the beach, they found Shalini basking in the sun.

"What's this?" their mother exclaimed, twitching her ears back and forth. "A little dragon! You're the first of your kind to visit us here, young sir!" Then, with a great deal of excited trumpeting and tail-swishing, Shoram and Shyla told her how they had heard the egg crack and found the little dragon just as he was hatching out, and how they had given him a name.

"Well, you clearly belong in our family," Shalini said warmly to Niji. She nuzzled him and her ears gave a big twitch.

"Mom, what do you know about these little dragons?" asked Shyla.

Shalini thought a moment and said, "Well, I think they come from the islands that the humans call Japan. I don't know how they made their way to this part of the world, but I do know they are usually quite shy—you don't see them very often. They lay their eggs near big dragon families like ours so the youngsters can be adopted by the big dragons. It's likely that Niji's mother had seen you and Shoram on Lookout Rock before. She must have believed you were both good and kind. She trusted you to take care of her baby, so she placed her egg where you'd be sure to find him."

Shyla said, "It's so cool, having a little brother. I'll bet he won't throw sand on me all the time like you do, Shoram!"

Shoram trumpeted once, then said, "I'll bet he's hungry. I'm going to get him some fish. Hatching must be a lot of work."

Shyla rolled her eyes. Her brother was always thinking about food! She stayed behind on the beach and chattered to her mother about all the things they could do together with Niji.

The little dragon loved the salmon that Shoram laid before him, even if Shoram did eat most of it. After they were both full, Niji let out a big yawn and began looking around for a nice place to curl up and take a nap. Shoram and Shyla arranged themselves around Niji so he was protected from the wind and from hungry eagles. Then they all snoozed peacefully in the afternoon sun.

A little while later they woke to the sound of Jaxon and Allie's voices. Shyla could hardly wait for the surprise on her human friends' faces when they saw the tiny newcomer.

Shyla wasn't disappointed. Allie and Jaxon came running across the beach, ready to play, but stopped short when they saw the tight bundle of dragons nestled in the sand. Allie saw Niji first. She just stood there, her mouth wide open. She didn't want to disturb him by being too loud.

"Is he asleep?" Allie whispered.

Stunned at the dragon's size, Jaxon said, "Is this little guy for real?"

Shyla lifted her head. "This," she said, swishing her tail carefully so as not to scare the little dragon, "is Niji. He just hatched out of his egg, over there on Lookout Rock." She pointed with her tail at the outermost sea stacks.

Niji looked up at Jaxon and Allie. "*Squeak, squeak,*" he said, which apparently meant *Nice to meet you.* Jaxon cupped his hands and held them out. To his delight Niji hopped right into his hands. Then Allie moved next to her brother and held her hands out, too, and Niji hopped over into Allie's hands. Niji began jumping up and down, digging in with his tiny claws.

"Hey, that tickles!" Allie laughed. Niji looked up in surprise as if to say, *What's the big deal? You wanted to be friends, didn't you?*

Suddenly they heard a loud roar. They looked up to see Shiran rushing out of his cave toward them. "Zorg is coming! And there's another dragon with him—Zonta, maybe. I'm sure they're after the fish we've stored in the tide pool. Jaxon and Allie, run quickly behind your log! And take the little dragon with you. Shoram and Shyla, into the water as we planned! Be ready to run up and help us surround them when they land."

Shoram and Shyla scrambled to follow their father's instructions. Soon they were almost completely submerged, only their nostrils visible above the rippling water. Jaxon and Allie, Niji still cushioned in Allie's hands, ran behind the big end of the magic log. Shiran and Shalini rushed back into their caves to wait. For a few seconds the beach was silent and empty. But in moments, Zorg, belching smoke and flapping his wings wildly, came swooping down around the rocks and landed on an open stretch of beach. Zonta landed much further away, looking a bit reluctant.

"What's going on? Where are they?" growled Zorg.

He swung his head back and forth, searching for a glimpse of bright dragon color and sniffing around for fish. When he caught the salmon scent, he headed for the pool with the Shi Shi dragons' fresh catch. Just as he was about to snatch up the fish, Shiran and Shalini came roaring out of their caves, as, at the same time, Shoram and Shyla burst out of the water. Seeing his dad was in trouble, Zonta rushed in to help. But it was too late—Zorg was surrounded. Zonta retreated to the rocks, letting out a worried whimper.

"So," roared Shiran, "you've come to steal our fish again, have you?"

"What of it?" Zorg snarled.

"Well, we're not going to let you do it. Catch your own fish—you know how. Why do you come here and cause trouble? Besides, you waste half of what you steal from us. It's no wonder your beach is called Stinky Fish Beach, with all those half-eaten fish lying around. I'm telling you, get out of here, *now*!" Shiran moved in close to Zorg and glared at him.

Zorg's face turned an angry red. Steam rolled out of his nose. His ears lay flat against the back of his head. But he knew he had to keep his temper and use his wits. Otherwise the Shi Shi dragons could trap him in one of their caves. *Who knows what they might do to me then?* he thought.

The children held their breath as they watched the stand-off: four fierce, brilliantly colored dragons surrounding one angry, gray-green dragon. Finally Shiran spoke in a deep voice. "Well? Are you going to leave? Is this to be the last of the fish stealing? Next time you come here, it'll be your turn to bring *us* some fish, I would think!"

Zorg took a deep breath and blew out a long snort of smoke. "I guess so," he said with a snarl. But really he was thinking, *I'll pretend to leave now, but I'll be back!* Zorg glanced over at the tide pool where the Shi Shi catch was stored.

"All right then," said Shiran, and the four Shi Shi dragons stepped back. In that instant Zorg stretched his neck out toward the pool and grabbed a great mouthful of fish. Immediately, the Shi Shi dragons jumped on him. They pinned Zorg's wings to the ground, and his face grew even redder.

Suddenly they saw a tiny blur of color whizzing around and squeaking, diving toward Zorg's head. "Niji, get back!" shouted Shyla.

"*Squeak! Squeak, squeak!*" Niji dove, burying his little teeth in the tender skin at the base of the gray-green dragon's ear.

Zorg roared and struggled, ears flapping, but he was firmly pinned. Niji dive-bombed Zorg again and again, nipping at his ears. Jaxon jumped up from behind the log, ready to head for the circle of dragons. His friends needed help!

"No, Jaxon, you can't!" Allie shouted. "And Niji shouldn't have gone in, either, but he's so fast, I couldn't stop him."

The beach was silent except for the snarls and steam coming from Zorg's mouth and nostrils. Even the gulls had disappeared. Finally, Shalini stretched out her long pink neck and said gently to Niji, "You must stop now. Come and rest on the top of my head."

The little rainbow dragon suddenly felt very tired. He flew up and perched on the bump of Shalini's broad forehead.

Shiran roared again, "Zorg, you lost your chance! Drop the fish and we'll let you go. Otherwise, things will only get worse for you." Zorg knew he had no choice. He dropped the fish, and Shoram carried them back to the tide pool.

The Shi Shi dragons moved back, much more slowly this time. Zorg got up and ambled off a little ways. He had pricking sensations all around his ears and stinging cuts in his wings from the claws of his foes. Slowly he crouched, spread his wings, and took off. Zonta quickly followed.

"Don't come back until you can bring some salmon to share! And stop bothering the animals on the beach!" the Shi Shi dragons roared. Niji added a few squeaks of his own for good measure. And they watched as Zorg and Zonta disappeared around the point.

Seven HOW TO BECOME INVISIBLE

Niji was settling very well into life with the Shi Shi dragons. He loved buzzing around their heads and distracting them while they napped in the sun. And he supplied an endless flutter of dragon squeaks about all sorts of things, particularly about Zorg. Shalini, especially, had a great fondness for the little dragon. She allowed him to perch on her forehead when they sat on the beach, watching the waves and admiring the sunsets.

Back at camp, Jaxon delved into to his dragon book with new interest. He learned that, indeed, there was a race of tiny dragons from Japan. "Allie," he said, "see this drawing? It looks just like Niji. And it says these small dragons are often found close to larger dragons, for protection. Just like here at Shi Shi."

He stared off into the distance, imagining dragons roaming the beaches of Japan.

Allie broke in, "What does it say about keeping them as pets? It'd be so cool if Niji could live with us in Seattle." Then she stopped herself, remembering little Niji nestled between Shalini's ears. He needed a dragon family.

Allie had tried to tell her mother about Niji and the scary encounter with Zorg, but Mom had only said, "That's pretty good, Allie. You two think up such great stories. Now go and get some firewood, please, so we can cook our breakfast." Allie raised her eyebrows at Jaxon. He grinned. Then they both took off, racing each other down the beach.

That morning was a foggy one. Mist swirled around the sea stacks and little fingers of fog curled in and out of the rock crevices. Down the beach at the dragon caves, Shyla was bored. She was flicking her tail around, playing tag with Niji. He was so fast that she couldn't tag him very often. Shoram joined in, too, and soon there was a flurry of iridescent colors, flicking tails, and showers of sand.

Then Shyla remembered something. "Let's see if we can make ourselves invisible! Then we can go over to Stinky Fish Beach and spy on Zorg and the others; see what they're up to."

"Good idea!" cried Shoram. "But how do we make ourselves invisible? Mom and Dad haven't taught us how to do that yet."

Shyla was pretty sure it had something to do with whistling the right note. Or was it a combination of notes? She began to whistle various notes and then a few tunes. As Shyla sang, she happened to hit a high C. And she disappeared!

"Whoa!" said Shoram. "Shyla, where'd you go?" Niji began to flit frantically about.

Then the green dragon and his tiny friend heard a giggle. "Right here, silly," said Shyla's voice.

"But I can't see you!" Niji squeaked.

"Well, why don't you try whistling and see if you can do it, too?" Shyla suggested.

Shoram started trying. He whistled notes, then sang dragon songs. He sang "Dragon Row the Boat Ashore" and "Hush Little Dragon." He sang "There Was an Old Dragon Who Swallowed His Fire" and all the other songs he could remember. This was getting discouraging! But Shoram kept going, until suddenly he hit a high C and *poof*!

Niji panicked. "I can't see anybody!" he squeaked.

"Don't worry, Niji, we're still here," said Shoram. "Just fly around until you bump into me. Then you can climb up on my back and ride to Stinky Fish Beach with us."

Just then Jaxon and Allie's voices echoed across the sand. The children could hear the young dragons, but where were they? And there was Niji, just sitting in thin air! "What's up, you guys?" Jaxon called out.

"We're invisible!" Jaxon recognized that trumpeting and knew at once it was Shoram.

"You guys are amazing!" said Allie. And as she walked forward, she nearly tripped as she bumped into something that felt solid as a tree.

"*Ow!*" cried Shyla. "You stepped on my tail!"

"Sorry," said Allie. "I didn't see you!"

"Oh yeah," Shyla giggled. "Hey, we're going over to Stinky Fish Beach to spy on the Zorgs. Mom and Dad wouldn't like it if we took you with us. But we'll come back and tell you all about it."

"Yeah, I guess so." Jaxon was disappointed, but he could always find something new in the tide pools, and Allie had her colored pencils to draw dragon pictures. "But hurry, okay?" he said. Stinky Fish Beach was further than their mom would have wanted them to go without an adult around.

So the young dragons, with Niji hunched down on Shoram's back, took off into the wind. Once they had flown around Lookout Rock they followed the coastline, flying low and slow. Soon they saw Zorg, Zorgina, and Zonta huddled around a fire on the littered beach.

"That must be it . . . Stinky Fish Beach," said Shyla.

"Yep," replied Shoram, flying in close to his sister. By now they could smell the rotting fish that had been left lying out on the sand. "Yuck! It sure deserves its name!"

They flew closer and circled, Shoram warning Niji to be very quiet. They listened to the dragons growling below them. "This fish is no good," they heard Zorg complain. "We need something fresh. Zonta, go on, get us some. I don't want to go over to Shi Shi today."

Zonta frowned. "You make me go fishing whenever you don't feel like stealing! You know how to fish. Why don't you go get some yourself? I'm going to hang out with my friends." Zonta stomped away from the fire.

"Dear . . ." said Zorgina, but she didn't finish. She looked into the fire and heaved a big, smoky sigh.

Shyla thought for a minute, then flew in just above Zorg's head and let out a low whistle. "What was that?" exclaimed Zorg angrily. Shyla flew a little way off and turned back, giving another whistle. Now Zonta and Zorgina were looking up, too, trying to figure out where the sound was coming from. Shyla flew around in large circles, whistling now and then, until they were thoroughly frustrated. Shoram, Niji still on his back, was sitting way back on the beach so that Niji's bright colors would be hidden in the bushes. Occasionally Niji squeaked, which confused Zorg and the others even more.

All this noise had awakened Zorg completely, and his hunger had made him impatient. "Guess I'll have to make the trip out to Shiran's for fish," he growled.

Shyla whistled out to Niji and Shoram, then waited to be sure they were within earshot.

"We'd better find a way to stop Zorg from stealing our fish!" said Shyla. "What can we do?" They could see the gray-green dragon stretching his wings, getting ready to fly.

"Quick, we need a plan!" Shyla cried.

Niji hopped up and down, and after listening to a series of noisy squeaks from the little dragon Shoram said, "Sounds good. Let's try it!"

Zorg launched into the air and was soon flying within a few feet of the invisible young dragons. Of course, Zorg didn't know that. He didn't even notice the bright rainbow-colored flashes as he passed the group.

That was the moment! Niji, being the fastest and quickest, flew directly at Zorg's head and began buzzing him like a mosquito. *What a crazy morning*, Zorg thought. And now this incessant noise around his head! Suddenly Zorg felt a nip at the bottom of his ear. *Ouch!* It was that dratted rainbow dragon that had come at his ears the other day! He roared and blew a burst of smoke. Niji kept up his buzzing and nipping, confusing the angry gray-green dragon so much that his wings began to falter.

At that moment the invisible dragons flew close, one on either side of Zorg. Then each of them let out a burst of fire, big enough to startle Zorg but not so big as to hurt Niji, who was still buzzing in circles. This was too much for Zorg. Fire out of a dragon's mouth was one thing, but two blasts of fire out of thin air? He was no match for that kind of magic. Zorg turned around right then and there.

Zorg's mood was now quite foul. He was hungry and tired and singed on both sides. He was so busy feeling sorry for himself that he didn't notice a little rainbow flash following along behind him. Niji had a new idea now, one he hadn't mentioned to Shoram or Shyla. So, while the two young dragons flew to Lookout Rock for a rest, Niji kept on going, following Zorg all the way back to his cave.

Shyla soon realized that Niji was missing.

"He's still following Zorg!" she exclaimed. She knew Niji wouldn't be able to fly such a long distance. The little dragon was fast at short sprints, but he tired easily. She saw Niji in the distance, beginning to weave and wobble in midair.

"I'm going to catch up with Niji and give him a ride," she told her brother.

"Good idea," said Shoram. "I'll follow you and keep an eye out for trouble."

As she took to the air, Shyla grew worried. She watched Niji falter again and again. He looked as though he might fall into the sea at any moment. Shyla flew faster—she willed herself to fly her fastest. Just when it seemed the tiny dragon couldn't fly another stroke, the invisible young dragon came up underneath Niji and caught him on her wing.

"Niji, it's me," Shyla said. "Can you climb onto my back? I'll take you the rest of the way to Stinky Fish Beach. But you have to tell me what you're up to, okay?"

"Thank you, thank you!" Niji chirped with relief. Slowly, the little dragon felt his way along Shyla's invisible wing until he reached her back and settled himself behind one of her spikes. Niji was glad to be safe and grateful for a chance to catch his breath.

Zorg landed near his campfire, ready to tear something apart. He growled at Zorgina and stomped around. He ran toward the seagulls that were pecking at his rotting fish and blew fire blasts at them. Seeing a raccoon that had come to the stream to drink, Zorg swatted at the animal with his powerful tail. Zonta and Zorgina managed to stay out of his way. Finally, Zorg grumbled away to his cave to sleep.

The invisible young dragons, with Niji hitchhiking on Shyla's back, landed atop the rocks that housed Zorg's cave. Niji took a quick snooze—he would need every bit of strength he could muster to carry out his plan. When the little dragon was ready, he took a deep breath, flashed a big smile, and zipped away toward the cave. He landed on Zorg's nose just as the grouchy dragon began snoring loudly.

Stinky breath! thought Niji. *Must be all that rotten fish he eats. Well, time to get busy.* With that, the tiny dragon nipped at Zorg's nostril. He flew upward a little way. Then Niji zipped downward and nipped one gray-green eyelid.

Zorg began to stir. "What's this?" he growled. His mood grew darker than ever. He looked up and saw a small rainbow dragon hovering above him, just out of reach.

"Oh it's you, is it!" Zorg roared. "Well, now you're going to be toast!" He took a deep breath and roared out a huge burst of fire. But Niji was much too quick for him and easily darted out of the way.

Zorg whirled around. Niji zoomed in and nipped the

bottom of the big dragon's ear. "*Yowch!*" yelled Zorg. Once again, Niji buzzed around and around in circles, evading the gray-green dragon. Zorg grew dizzy trying to catch the fast little fellow.

A moment later Zorg erupted from his cave, flapping madly every which way, swatting at Niji with his wings. Niji was in fine form now, thoroughly enjoying himself as he darted in for quick nips at Zorg's head. The small dragon was having so much fun that he didn't see the enormous gray shadow coming down on him. Suddenly he was trapped on the ground under Zorg's dark, smelly wing.

"Got you! And just when I thought there was nothing to eat!" Zorg snorted.

Niji searched for patches of light. He tried to slip out under the edges here and there, but each time Zorg flattened his wing to the ground to keep the little dragon pinned. Niji tried nipping at Zorg's wing, but no luck. A dragon's wing-skin is tough, and Zorg didn't feel a thing. Niji tried buzzing and tickling. That didn't work, either, and he was getting tired. Zorg kept drawing his wing in closer and closer to his body. Soon the tiny dragon would be close to his foot. Then Zorg would be able to seize little Niji in his sharp claws and pop him into his mouth! "*Mmmmm, toasted baby dragon,*" Zorg gloated. "This is going to be good!" A long drizzle of saliva dripped from his jaws.

Perched atop the sea stack, Shoram and Shyla couldn't make out what was happening. They expected Niji to appear at any minute, so they waited.

But Niji was beginning to panic. Nothing he tried was working. And Zorg's wing kept closing in tighter and tighter. Then suddenly Niji remembered the tender fold of skin right where the dragon's wing joined his body. Niji flew straight up into the big dragon's wingpit and gave it a fierce bite.

"*Yikes!*" cried Zorg. He flapped open his wing to stop the stinging. In a flash Niji zipped out. Fresh air! He flew straight to the top of the rock.

Zorg roared and roared, wild with anger

as he watched his meal escaping. Niji hovered about the tall rock squeaking nervously, so scared he forgot that his friends couldn't be seen. "Where are you guys?" he chirped.

"Over here," Shyla whispered. She tried to purr reassuringly like her mother did. Niji flew around until he bumped into Shyla. He landed on her back with a sigh of relief.

"Let's get out of here!" said Shyla. Niji squeaked in agreement.

"Right," said Shoram. The group took off, climbing quickly into the sky. Below, they could see Zorg still waving his front legs and roaring furiously at the air.

They soon arrived back at Shi Shi. Niji was still quivering with fear and excitement. He squeaked out his story again and again, and with each retelling the fierce dragon's wing got bigger and darker. Shiran had gone fishing, but Shalini, Jaxon, and Allie listened enthralled. Niji's escape was a narrow one, indeed!

But now Shoram and Shyla had a dilemma.

"Mom, we need you," they called out to Shalini. "Can you help us be visible again?"

"Well now, let me see . . ." mused Shalini, her eyes twinkling. "I might have to go and consult the seaweed oracle on that one. . . ."

"You mean you don't *know*?" asked the worried voices. Both Shyla and her brother were more than ready to be normal again. But Shalini had already hurried off to her seaweed oracle and turned to the orange and magenta pages where the necessary instructions were written.

"Ah yes," she murmured, her ears twitching as she made her way back to the young dragons. "This time you must whistle as low as you can, down to a low C."

Shyla and Shoram tried various notes, each time whistling a note lower than the last. With each note he whistled, it seemed to the children that their young friend Shoram was sinking further and further into the sand. Then *poof!* The young dragon was back in all his shimmery emerald greenness.

"Wow!" said Allie and Jaxon at once.

Shyla frowned at her brother (although no one saw her) then whistled even lower, her eyes nearly crossing with the effort. At last she popped into view once more, with all her purples and glistening gold.

"Thanks Mom," said Shyla, turning to her mother as her tail flicked into an attractive curve.

"Yeah Mom, thanks," said Shoram. He turned to Jaxon and Allie. "You know, being invisible's not all that great. It gets old pretty fast. I'll probably give it up after this." He trumpeted for emphasis. Shalini laughed, grateful her little ones were safe.

"Well, if anyone in this family does decide to become invisible in the future," said the mother dragon, "you might want to ask for a little help." She flicked her ears as Niji nuzzled her. "Just in case."

eight THE COLOR-CHANGING POOL

It was late afternoon. Niji was asleep, his head nestled in a patch of shady moss atop a sea stack near the dragon caves. Shoram and Shyla were up the beach a short way, digging in the sand, trying to see who could find the tastiest clams for a snack. As the two dragons worked to dig a deep hole, they noticed water rushing into it. The water had a special quality to it—as if it contained slivers of bright metal. The breeze played on the water, making it move and swirl like the threads of fog that danced through the early morning air on Shi Shi. At once Shyla thought of Allie, sure that her human friend would love creating a picture of this extraordinary pool. The young purple dragon swished the tip of her tail into the silvery water, playing with the light. She watched in amazement as some of her scales changed color. The tip of her tail had turned completely golden!

Shoram pushed his sister a little, trumpeting excitedly. "Hey, let me try!" He pushed his front leg deep into the water. The scales turned blue! The young dragon waved his blue leg in the air. "Look! Just like Dad's!" Shoram had always thought of his father's blue skin as a mark of strength.

"Wow," he said, "I wonder what'd happen if I jumped all the way into the pool. Would I turn blue all over?"

"Well," Shyla said, admiring her golden tail tip, "we'll have to dig a deeper hole if you want to go that far." She flourished her tail in the air, then drew an S in the sand. "Yes!" she said. "Let's do it!"

So they set about digging. And the pool got bigger and bigger.

"Ready, set!" said Shoram, and then trumpeted, "here I go!" In he went, water splashing all around him. The pool closed over Shoram until the only thing Shyla could see were her brother's two green nostrils.

Under the water, Shoram heard a deep voice. "What color

do you wish to be?" Shoram looked up through the water's surface. Only Shyla there. Since when did pools talk? But Shoram was so excited about changing color that he didn't stop to think for very long before he made his choice.

"Blue," he said. "I want to be blue, like Dad."

"Blue it shall be," the pool intoned.

Shoram's skin begin to prickle and tickle. He lifted his head from the water and looked down. He was blue all over! He jumped out of the pool to admire himself. His scales were a wonderful rich aqua, not quite like Dad's deep blue. But close enough!

"Wow, Shoram!" Shyla cried. "What a color! But the inside of your nostrils is still green!" She leaned in close to see all the new colors her brother was wearing.

"Oh, that's the part that didn't go under," Shoram laughed. Now he was a two-tone dragon!

"And your spikes are still red," Shyla pointed out.

"Well, that way I definitely won't get confused with Dad," replied Shoram. Both dragons twisted and turned in the sunlight to admire Shoram's new shades of blue.

"My turn now!" said Shyla excitedly, her tail dancing in the air. "Let's see—what color do I want to be? *Hmm . . .* I think I'd like to be gold all over!" She liked the way her golden tail tip caught the light.

Shyla jumped into the pool of silvery water and ducked down until she was sure her whole body was covered. She heard the pool ask, "And what color would you like to be, young Shyla?"

She was surprised to hear her name. "Gold, please."

"Gold and silver are reserved for dragons of great merit," the pool said. "Have you developed your great qualities?"

Shyla stopped to think. What did it mean to be a dragon of great merit? She had always been generous in sharing her fish. She helped her brother calm down when he got a little wild and trumpeted too much. She had helped her parents teach the Zorg dragons a lesson. And she watched out for Jaxon and Allie when they came to Shi Shi. All of this seemed to indicate that, indeed, she was a dragon of no small merit. Shyla raised her nostrils out of the water and took a deep breath. "Yes," she said, gathering her confidence. "I think so, yes. I've developed . . . qualities." She smiled politely underwater. Could the pool see her?

Shoram piped up, "That's right, she's been good . . . even if she is my sister."

"I see," said the pool. Shyla sat deep in the water, still waiting. Then suddenly she felt her skin begin to prickle and tickle, and she had to resist the giggles. When she looked down she saw that she was all golden . . . shiny, shiny golden. But her nostrils remained the beautiful purple color they had always been. She stepped gracefully from the water, arching her neck to admire the scales at the base of her golden-yellow spikes. *I'm the color of the sunshine,* she thought happily, and skipped a few steps around the pool.

"Wow, cool!" exclaimed Shoram. "Let's go show Mom and Dad."

"But what about the pool?" Shyla asked with a final shake of her tail. "Should we just leave it here?" They turned and saw to their surprise that the silvery water was spreading into the sand and the hole was quickly disappearing. Shyla felt a moment of sadness. It was such wonderful magic and it had departed so quickly. But her brother's excitement was contagious as he flapped his wings and hopped with glee in all directions before heading back to the family's caves. Shyla hurried to catch up with him.

Just down the beach Allie was sitting by herself on the magic log, busy with her drawing pad and pencils. Back at camp her brother was busy whittling a dragon from a piece of driftwood, so Allie had come out to the beach to do some sketches. She was startled and a little frightened when she saw the aqua-blue and the golden dragons cavorting their way toward her. She heard a trumpeting that sounded just like Shoram, but where were his bright green scales? And that glorious sunshine-gold dragon . . . could that be Shyla?

"Allie, it's us!" It was the aqua-blue dragon, punctuating his cry with a loud trumpet across the sand.

"Yep, it's us!" added the golden dragon, skipping, hopping, and swishing her tail.

They sounded and acted like her friends, but Allie still wasn't sure. She stayed on the log and watched. *I wish Jaxon were here,* she thought. *He's not going to believe this!*

Shoram and Shyla hurried to the dragon caves to find their parents. For these young dragons, running usually meant taking several steps and hops, then a few wing flaps to give speed, and a few more hops and quick steps. The brother and sister dragon were back at the caves in no time at all. Shalini saw them first. Then Niji hopped down from his perch on the rock and flew to safety between Shalini's ears. He wasn't so sure about these new dragons, either.

"Well, what have we here?" Shalini asked. "Are these two young dragon strangers, come to visit?"

"Don't you know us?" tooted Shoram.

Shyla arched her neck and swished her tail at the same time, so that her scales glittered brightly in the sunshine. "It's us, Mom, really!"

"*Hmm . . .* " Shalini teased, twitching her ears. "And who is *us*, exactly?"

"You know, *us*!" Shoram and Shyla shouted. "See! Look at our nostrils! And our spikes!" They were beginning to feel a bit distressed.

As if I wouldn't know my own children, Shalini smiled to herself. She bent nearer and pretended to look closely at each of them. "Why, so it is you!" she laughed. "It seems you two found the magic pool."

Niji squeaked and bounced about on Shalini's head, but still he didn't fly to the aqua-blue or the golden dragon. Niji listened closely as Shyla and Shoram spoke; he was still getting used to their new colors.

"You *know* about the magic pool?" Shyla asked, surprised.

"Why, yes, I do—but it only works on dragons of exceptional merit." She blew a gentle steam ring and glanced at Shoram. He squirmed a little in his new aqua skin.

"The pool lets you become gold or silver if you have a whole lot of merit!" Shyla added, her tail dancing on the sand.

Shalini smiled. "Of course, merit includes humility—not boasting about your good qualities . . ."

"Uh-huh," agreed Shyla, her tail calming a bit as she thought this over.

"Hey, Mom, why don't you and Dad come and change colors, too?" said Shoram. "Then we could all fool Zorg— he'd never recognize us."

"Well, I'm not sure it would fool him for long, but it would be fun to have a change of color," said his mother.

Shalini called to Shiran, who in a moment emerged slowly and sleepily from his cave.

"We're going to the magic pool to change colors," she said. "We'd like it if you came along." Shiran agreed. Niji went along, too, but the little dragon insisted he would stay as he was. He liked his rainbow scales just fine.

Shoram and Shyla led the way. Shiran and Shalini hadn't dug out the magic pool in many years and were surprised the young ones had found it. Clearly their offspring were smart young dragons. The parents knew also that the magic pool had a way of appearing on its own when the time was right. Perhaps the pool would help them deal with Zorg.

The digging went very fast with all four of them working, even with the young dragons stopping occasionally to check their bright new scales and skin. To cover great Shiran, they had to dig a very big hole indeed. But soon the pool was large enough, and they watched as the silvery water again formed its luminous patterns.

Further down the beach Allie was still seated on the magic log. She looked up from her drawing. What was it the dragons were doing out there on the sand? She put away her Shyla-purple pencil, as well as the Zorg-green. Then she tucked her sketchbook under her arm and moved closer to watch. She didn't want to disturb the dragons' family time, but she was curious.

Suddenly Shalini blew the biggest steam ring she'd created all summer. "I've got an idea!"

"Imagine this," she said, her ears twitching excitedly. "Shiran, let's switch colors—I'll become blue and you can turn pink. That way we can confuse Zorg the next time he comes to make trouble."

Shiran nodded slowly. The more he thought about it, the more he liked the idea. He slipped into the silvery water, thinking, *Pink, pink, pink* . . . And because his mind was strong and wise, his thoughts were so clear that the pool didn't even need to ask his color wishes. He felt his skin starting to prickle and tickle. When he looked down into the water again, his scales and skin were indeed pink.

But Shiran had not become an ordinary shade of pink. Instead of Shalini's deep magenta, the great male dragon was a deep coral-pink, glowing almost golden in the late afternoon light. Shyla thought she'd never seen any color more beautiful than her golden scales, but her father's new colors were magnificent! And with pink spikes, too! As had happened for Shoram and Shyla, Shiran's nostrils were still blue. And his family was glad for that. They could get up close and see right away that, yes, it was still Shiran: blue nostrils, and wisdom shining in his eyes.

After a few quiet minutes, while everyone thought about how mighty Shiran looked in his color change, they turned to Shalini.

"Your turn, m'lady," Shiran said. Niji hopped and flapped down from the mother dragon's head and perched on Shoram.

Shalini slid into the silver water repeating to herself, *Blue, blue, blue* . . . Her thoughts, too, were strong and clear, and the pool knew exactly what to do. The silver water prickled and tickled her sides until her skin itched a little and . . . Shyla gasped! Her mother looked so different, her scales now a deep violet blue. But there were the telltale magenta nostrils, and that made Shyla feel better.

"I think your idea may, in fact, work very well, Shoram," said his mother as she moved onto the packed sand near the pool. "Right now it's not easy for the five of us to remember who's who. So just imagine what Zorg may think!" She smiled and shook a little, sending a sprinkling of silvery water over the others.

Shiran looked thoughtful. "Some adjustments are in order," he said. "I think Shyla's brilliant gold color might alert Zorg that something is up. Perhaps you should choose a color that doesn't gleam quite so brightly," he said to his daughter.

Now, Shyla did not want to change colors—she loved being golden. But gold was reserved for meritorious dragons. And that meant working with the rest of her family to get Zorg to change his ways. Yes, Shyla thought, maybe they could help Zorg become less grumpy and lazy (and stop stealing fish).

"Okay," said Shyla, "then I'll change to . . ." She gazed off at the ocean and thought of the colorful seaweeds. "How about green with orange spots?" she offered, her tail gently twitching.

"*Hmm*," Shalini said. "Later perhaps, but right now that would be a bit too noticeable." Niji squeaked in agreement.

"I know!" said Shyla. "I'll ask the magic pool what color I should be." Shalini smiled at her daughter's growing wisdom.

Shyla jumped into the silvery water. She waited until she heard the pool ask, "What color would you like to be?"

"Magic pool," Shyla said, "I'd like to change to a color that will help us catch Zorg, so we can help him mend his ways."

"Very well," said the pool, and Shyla felt her skin prickling and changing. She saw that she had become a vivid orchid, quite different from her father's new coral-pink. Shyla felt a twinge of sadness until she caught sight of the very tip of her tail. It was still golden! As she came out of the water she gave it a swish. She turned to look at her back. Her spikes had stayed golden, as well.

"Well, Shyla," said her mother with a twitch of her ears, "it seems the pool recognized your unselfish concern for our cause. Perhaps now we can help Zorg stop his foolishness so he can get along better with others."

In the dragons' excitement, none of them noticed that Allie had slipped off the log and headed back to camp. *I'm not telling Jaxon about this color-changing business,* thought Allie. *He wouldn't believe me anyway. He'll just have to see for himself!*

nine RED HEART ROCK POWER

It was the children's last day on the beach. Well, thought Allie, at least Mom had promised they would come back again in a couple of weeks—one last camping trip before school started. Allie and Jaxon were determined to spend the day with the dragons before going back to Seattle.

As they walked down to the point, the children kept their eyes on the beach. You never knew when you might find a special stick, an unusual beach rock, maybe even an agate. Once they got home, Jaxon thought, it would be fun to show Dad their rocks, to hear him explain the origin of each one.

"Look at this cool red heart-shaped rock, Jaxon!" Allie called out. Her brother came over and studied the small stone in her hand. "Maybe this is some of the jasper Dad told us about, remember?"

A few minutes later Jaxon made a discovery. "Look at these cool green rocks. Maybe they're jade." By the time they reached the magic log, both of Allie's pockets and Jaxon's, too, were bulging with interesting rocks.

Jaxon and Allie emptied out their collections and spread them on a flat spot on the log. The children sat sorting through their rocks as they kept an eye out for the dragons. Sure enough, they soon heard Niji's character-istic squeaks.

"*Squeak, squeak, squeak-a-squeak!*" Niji buzzed around Allie's head and landed on Jaxon's shoulder. "Have you seen? The big dragons have all changed colors! First it was Shoram and Shyla." He was buzzing and squeaking so fast that Jaxon and Allie could hardly understand him. "Nobody told me they were going to do that. When I woke up from a nap, I didn't know who they were! What if my family had gone away and strangers had found me?"

"Niji, we'd never do that," said orchid-pink Shyla with the golden spikes and tail tip. She walked up to the log, flip-ping her tail to emphasize the point.

Jaxon looked at Shyla wide-eyed. "Wow, is that you?" he asked. Bright rays of light bounced off Shyla's golden spikes as she moved. Then an aqua-blue dragon came running up, and his trumpeting gave him away. "Hey, it's you, buddy!" added Jaxon. "Those green nostrils look awesome with those blue scales and red spikes!"

Shoram preened and strutted. "Thanks," he said. "I kinda like it myself."

"Where are Shiran and Shalini?" asked Allie.

"Oh, they've gone fishing," said Shyla.

"Want to help us look for special rocks?" said Allie. "There's a certain kind of rock that . . . if we can find some, they might help you fight Zorg." She dug into her pockets.

"See?" Allie added, showing them a rock she had found on the beach. It was a dark burnished red. "Let's find more of these red heart-shaped ones."

"Sure!" said Shoram, intrigued.

"What do they do?" Shyla asked. "It just looks like a little red rock to me."

"I'll show you later," said Allie. "Let's start looking."

Everyone, including Niji, began searching for the special rocks. There was a dark cave near the log that, the young Shi Shi dragons explained, had once been a dragon cave. Now it was full of sea life and showed no signs of dragon use. The caves of the Shi Shi dragons were further out toward Lookout Rock, where they could keep watch over the beach. There they could see any creature approaching, whether by land, sea, or air.

As they explored the cave's entrance, they found all sorts of interesting things: fish bones, a few feathers, delicate sea shells, even a sea urchin half hidden under the edge of a large rock.

"What're these?" asked Jaxon. He held up two slender disks so thin you could almost see through them, and smooth as mother-of-pearl.

"Oh, those are just old dragon scales," said Shoram, not a

bit interested. But he was quite impressed with the large, sharp bear teeth that Allie found. With some effort, the group turned up several more red heart-shaped rocks, worn smooth by the tidewaters. Allie held up a couple of small rocks flecked with glittery bits that caught the sunlight.

"Fool's gold," said Jaxon. "I have some of this stuff at home."

"Can I have them?" asked Shyla, who loved all things golden.

"Sure," said Allie. "For the plan I have in mind, all we need are these red heart rocks."

"Could I have the bear's teeth?" asked Shoram. Allie smiled yes, and handed them over.

Not to be outdone by the bigger dragons, Niji collected several feathers. Unlike rocks and bear teeth, these were light enough for him to carry.

Jaxon couldn't stand it any longer. He pulled Allie aside. "So what's this big plan?"

"Nope," said Allie. "Not 'til later. You'll see how it works." Jaxon wasn't sure about his sister's secrecy, but he decided now wasn't the time to argue.

With a red heart rock in each pocket, Jaxon and Allie followed Shoram and Shyla back to their caves to put away their new-found treasures. Just as they arrived at the shoreline, two great dragons came out of the water, each with a mouthful of salmon, fish heads and tails poking out like whiskers. Jaxon gasped!

Shalini chuckled. Again, that wonderful sound of cymbals. The great blue dragon lowered her head to put her fish into the pool. "Jaxon," she said, "you look confused. Don't worry, we just made a little change. Now I'm blue and Shiran is pink."

Jaxon took a minute for this to sink in. *Opposite*, he thought. Each of the parent dragons was the color that the *other* one had been before. *Opposite, opposite, opposite.*

It wasn't easy for Jaxon to keep all this sorted out, especially with Niji now sitting on his shoulder, squeaking excitedly in his ear. *What could Allie have in mind?* he wondered, thinking of the heart-shaped rocks. But Niji's squeak was insistent.

"Not so loud, Niji!" complained Jaxon. "I'm right here!"

"*Squeak, squeak, SQUEAK!*" yelled Niji as he flew up toward Lookout Rock.

"Not good," said Shiran. Sure enough, as he peered into the sky, a familiar dark shape was flying toward the group. "It looks like Zorg's back. Shoram and Shyla, to your caves. Jaxon and Allie, over there behind your log." Dragons and children moved quickly.

"Jaxon, your cap!" Allie cried. Her brother scooped up his soccer cap as the two of them rushed across the sand.

"Come on, Allie. What about the plan?"
he hissed in her ear.

"Okay, listen," she said. "Zorg is probably going to land

close to the pool. Then he'll come looking for everyone. Shiran will come running out of his cave, but he'll be pink, so Zorg will think Shiran is Shalini. He's not so scared of her, so he'll probably figure he can just grab the fish and get away with it because no one else is around. Then Niji will come in dive-bombing . . ." Allie was focused, watching the scene unfold in her mind.

"And that's where we come in, right?" Jaxon guessed.

"Right." Allie had known her brother would catch on fast. "Just as Zorg takes off with his mouth full of fish, you and I come running out from behind this log. Then you take your soccer cap and throw it over Zorg's eyes. Niji will come in from underneath and nip at Zorg's wingpits. Zorg will try to get away, and if Niji keeps nipping at him, eventually he'll flip over. Then, if we're lucky, Zorg will fall on his back." Allie was breathless, speaking as fast as she could. Jaxon had never seen her so intent on anything.

She dug into her pocket, pulled out a red heart rock, and held it up. "Before he can turn himself over, we've got to run up and throw these at the spot right in the center of his chest. If we aim really well, the rocks will strike the one soft spot on a dragon."

"What'll that do?" Jaxon asked.

"It's supposed to affect his heart . . . and change it for the better," Allie said.

"I'm impressed, Sis," said Jaxon. "How'd you come up with all that?"

"The other day while you were carving driftwood, I looked into your book about dragons. It says a dragon has a soft spot in the center of his heart area. Dragons are really vulnerable there—they can be brought down by arrows or swords aimed at that spot. I'm hoping the red heart rocks will touch Zorg's heart and help him change his ways. But I'm pretty sure it will only work if they hit that soft spot. I talked to Niji and Shiran about it at the cave, and they said they knew some of the rocks on the beach had charms in them, but they weren't sure which ones. They thought the plan was worth a try." Jaxon fingered his red rock and snugged his soccer cap firmly on his head.

"Okay, I'm in," he said.

Just as Allie had predicted, Zorg soon landed by the fish storage pool and began searching for the Shi Shi dragons. They could see Niji buzzing nearby high in the air, unnoticed by the gray-green dragon. And just as planned, Shiran came roaring out of the cave in all his coral-pink glory. Zorg looked puzzled for an instant, then thrust out his chest with a gravelly laugh.

"You think you can stop me, Shalini?" At that moment Niji came zooming in, nipping at Zorg's ear. "Dratted little dragon. . . . Get ready to be lizard toast!" Zorg yelled. He grabbed a mouthful of fish, took off into the air, and turned to challenge Niji.

"Jaxon, *now!*" shouted Allie.

Jaxon ran out from behind the log and, taking careful aim, threw his soccer cap at Zorg's head. But Zorg turned unexpectedly. The cap hooked itself onto a horn and covered Zorg's left eye. "*Aaaargh!*" he yelled. He could see out of only one eye. *Which way?* he thought, frantically. *The*

pesky little gnat! I'll tear his wings off and . . . Niji was still nipping away at Zorg, who couldn't bite back because his mouth was full of fish.

Niji's movements were so fast they made Zorg dizzy. The little dragon flew beneath and behind him, back and forth, up and down, and then began nipping at his wing-pits. This drove Zorg wild! He batted his wings, trying to push Niji out. But Zorg only ended up confusing himself. Desperately, he heaved his great body in an airborne somersault, and crash-landed on his back on the rocks.

"*Yowch!* You little monster! I'll . . ." he snarled through his mouthful of fish. He was not going to let go of those fish!

"The rocks!" yelled Allie. She and Jaxon sprinted up to Zorg. "Take your best shot!" she shouted. She and Jaxon each grabbed one of their red heart-shaped rocks and threw as hard as they could. They watched, panting, as both rocks hit the soft spot in the center of Zorg's chest with a satisfying thud.

At once Zorg stopped moving. The children froze.

"Allie . . ." whispered Jaxon. "Zorg . . . Do you think we killed him?"

"No," said Allie. "Look, he's still breathing. But look, Jaxon!" As the two watched in astonishment, the soft spot on Zorg's chest began to glow a rosy pink, in strong contrast to the dull gray-green scales on his belly. The rosy spot on Zorg's chest began pulsating. It grew brighter and more vivid. The dragon remained motionless on the sand.

Shalini, Shoram, and Shyla had come out of their caves.

The group stood around Zorg in amazement. Niji hopped and flapped and took his place on Shalini's forehead.

"I think those red rocks did have an effect," said Allie. But before Jaxon could answer, the rosy spot on Zorg's chest began to fade again, growing paler and greener. Zorg began to struggle in an attempt to turn himself over onto his feet.

Shiran approached. "Stand back, everyone," he said quietly. "Something has happened to Zorg. We need to let him go now. Let's just wait a few days and see what happens."

"But he sure can't take our fish," grumbled Shoram. Shyla looked at her brother and back at Zorg, who was now standing before the group.

The gray-green dragon looked dazed. He regarded each of them slowly. Zorg dropped the fish and tossed his head as if to shake off a dream. One final shake and Zorg seemed to be himself again. "Clearly outnumbered," he snarled, glancing darkly at Niji. And there was that human with the cap, holding a handful of rocks. Zorg decided it would be best to make his exit.

The Shi Shi dragons and the children stepped back. Zorg, still shaking his head a little, crouched and took off, but his roar sounded a bit muffled. As he flew, he thought, *I'm not coming back here for a while. Those humans know too much.*

The mood on Shi Shi Beach was thoughtful as they watched Zorg fly away. Even Niji was quieter than usual. The big dragons turned to Jaxon and Allie.

"Thank you so much for your help," Shalini said softly. "You know, I expect we're going to see a change in Zorg." She remembered the old stories she had heard as a young dragon, about the power of the red heart rocks to make important changes. Shiran agreed. Shoram and Shyla hardly heard their parents. They were still thinking about that glowing, pulsating spot on Zorg. Shoram looked down at his own chest to see if he could find his own soft spot.

Jaxon and Allie glanced at each other silently. Both felt a quiet thrill, certain that the plan had worked. Now they really didn't want to leave the beach.

"I guess we won't see you again for a while," said Allie. "We're going home tomorrow." Her heart felt soft and sad. "What will happen when Zorg comes back? We won't be here to help you."

"You mustn't worry, dear," said Shalini, bringing her head down close to Allie's and flicking her ears. "That old fellow won't be coming back for a while. And before you know it, you'll be back with us on Shi Shi beach."

Jaxon looked up at the sky. The sun was sinking low and the clouds had begun to glow with twilight oranges and pinks. He spoke quietly. "We'd better go now, Allie. Mom's going to worry if we aren't back soon." The two hugged each of the dragon's necks, Allie wiped away a few tears, and they turned to go. Jaxon and Allie walked without a word, each one fingering a red heart-shaped rock as they made their way back to camp.

ten DRAGON SOCCER

Jaxon and Allie had been back at their house in Seattle for a couple of weeks. Jaxon studied the details of his dragon book and Allie practiced her dragon paintings, but neither of them were having much fun. They missed Shi Shi terribly.

"It's just not the same here," Allie said as they lay on the grass in the backyard one afternoon. "I wonder what Shoram and Shyla are doing right now. And what do you suppose Zorg is up to since we hit that soft spot over his heart?" She reached into her pocket and wrapped her fingers around a red heart-shaped rock. She now carried it everywhere, placing it under her pillow at night when she went to sleep.

Jaxon's dragon bone was now his most prized possession.

His Dad had taken it to some professor friends at the college and they couldn't identify it, so Jaxon was even more convinced it was from an ancient dragon. He kept it on the shelf over his bed. And every day Jaxon took his own red rock from his dresser and tucked it into his pants pocket.

"We just have to find a way to get back to the beach," he agreed.

At dinner that night they were surprised to hear Mom say, "Only two more weeks until school starts, kids. I promised you we'd have one more trip out to Shi Shi before that. And we'd better do it soon, because the fall rains are sure to be coming any day now."

"Yes!" shouted Jaxon. "Can we go tomorrow?"

"I'll start packing tonight!" added Allie excitedly.

"I can't go until the weekend," they heard Dad say. "I have some meetings at the college to get ready for fall term."

"Well, how about we go this Thursday and make it an

extra long weekend?" Mom suggested. Dad agreed, and Jaxon and Allie set about planning what they would take with them, and what they might do with the dragons on this last visit.

The next couple of days seemed to drag on endlessly, but on Thursday morning they were all ready at last. Jaxon put his dragon bone in the large pocket of his backpack, together with his dragon book. And this time he would take his soccer ball, repaired and almost as good as new. Allie had packed up her colored pencils and her sketchbook, which was now full of pictures of dragons in various poses, as well as scenes of their beach adventures.

When they arrived at Shi Shi late that afternoon, they found their old campsite was still there, complete with shelter logs, fire ring, and little table. Jaxon and Allie dropped their backpacks and started running down to the point.

"Not so fast, guys!" Dad called out. "We need to get the tarp up for the shelter. And we need help gathering firewood for tonight. You can go down there after dinner."

"*Aww,*" Jaxon said, turning around reluctantly. "Allie, you have to come back, too," he added. He wasn't about to let Allie get to the dragons first.

"I'm *coming*!" Allie said, turning to follow Jaxon.

Soon dinner was ready. After gulping down their plates of spaghetti, the two of them ran as fast as they could down to the magic log. They took their seats on the big end and tried to be patient, but the dragons were nowhere in sight. No Shoram, no Shyla, no Niji. No one.

"Where are they?" Allie whispered.

"I dunno," Jaxon said glumly. "Let's just wait a little longer." He looked into the distance.

"Do you think they're invisible right now?" Allie suggested.

"Maybe." Jaxon didn't sound hopeful.

They waited on the log for a long time, but the dragons didn't appear. One by one stars appeared in the sky, and the breeze off the water became chilly. Neither of them wanted to give up and go back to camp.

At last Jaxon said, "Maybe we should just go back to camp and come back in the morning."

"I hope they haven't gone away for good." Allie was holding back tears. She clutched her red rock tightly as she and her brother walked slowly back to camp, looking over their shoulders every now and then, just in case.

It was a restless night for Jaxon and Allie. They woke up with every sound near camp—raccoons rummaging around their food table, chipmunks running up and down the log near their heads, an owl hooting persistently. Even the gentle sound of the surf couldn't lull them back to sleep. At one point Allie was sure she heard a dragon roar. But then maybe it was just a big wave, she thought, breaking on the shore.

The tide was way out when they woke up the next morning. After a quick breakfast of granola, they were off at a dead run down to the point. Once up on the magic log they surveyed the open expanse of sand and rocks in front of them. Where were the dragons?

Suddenly Jaxon pointed. "Look, there's Niji!" Allie spotted Niji's frenzied little rainbow wings buzzing around the entrance to a cave.

"And Shiran!" cried Allie as the dragon's majestic coral-pink form emerged from his cave. Shalini, Shoram, and Shyla weren't far behind.

"They're all there!" cried Jaxon, as both of them hopped off the log and ran over to the dragons.

"We came down here last night. Where were you guys?" asked Allie.

Shalini regarded the children thoughtfully. She blew a gentle steam ring. "Some things are better left as mysteries," she said seriously.

Allie knew better than to keep asking questions. "I'm so glad to see you," she said to Shyla. "I was worried that you'd gone away!" Allie gave Shyla a big hug. The young dragon swished her tail playfully and curved her long orchid-colored neck close around Allie's slender body. Jaxon jumped on Shoram's back and they half-flew, half-hopped around in a happy circle.

"Great to see you again, buddy!" Jaxon exclaimed. Niji was so happy to see the family's human friends that he flew round and around, squeaking loudly, until finally he settled on Jaxon's shoulder.

"Hey, cool, you guys!" Allie laughed. "You're like a dragon-human pyramid!"

Just then Shalini called out to them. "We should do some fishing!" Then, seeing Shoram and Shyla so happily cavorting with Jaxon and Allie again, she added, "Oh, that's all right. I can catch some fish for you two if you want to play for a while."

"Thanks, Mom!" called Shoram. Allie and Shyla were busy catching up, when Jaxon broke in.

"What's Zorg been up to?" he asked.

"We haven't seen him at all," Shoram replied. "Well, once he did come around but he didn't make any trouble. He just landed a little way off and stomped around for a while. He chased some seagulls. And then he flew away. We haven't had a single fish stolen since you guys used those red rocks on him."

Just then Niji interrupted, "*Squeak, squeak . . . squeak!*" he said. "Look up, there's someone coming!"

They all looked. There was a dot in the sky growing larger and nearer. "Maybe Zorg is coming, after all," Jaxon said excitedly. *I'd like to throw my dragon bone at his soft spot and see what'd happen then,* he thought. Jaxon figured it was probably magical, too, being the bone of a magical creature. But then he realized he might risk losing his talisman, and decided against it.

"Nope, that's not big enough to be Zorg," observed Shoram. They all watched as the dull green Zonta landed on the beach in front of them.

"Hey, Zonta. We haven't seen you in a while. What brings you here?" asked Shoram. He wondered if maybe Zorg had sent his dragon son to spy on the Shi Shi dragons.

The children stood very still.

"Well," replied Zonta, "I was wondering if you'd help me do some fishing. Ever since my dad was hit on his soft spot he hasn't wanted to come and steal fish. He still won't go fishing himself, though, even when I offer to go with him. I know how to fish okay, but you guys know where all the biggest salmon hang out, and I was hoping you could show me. We could all get some for ourselves. And then I could take some back for Mom and Dad."

Shoram and Shyla exchanged glances—they'd been looking forward to playing with Jaxon and Allie. Then Jaxon had an idea.

"Sure, why don't you guys all go fishing," he said. "Allie and I will stay here, and when you come back I'll show you all a fun game."

"What are you up to?" Allie whispered.

"You'll see, Sis," said Jaxon.

The young Shi Shi dragons decided that fishing with Zonta couldn't hurt. They were hungry for breakfast, after all, and their mother hadn't yet returned with any fish. Shoram and Shyla found a spot for Niji on a tall rock where he could watch them.

"Stay right here, Niji. Mom will be back soon, and then so will we," said Shyla. Then she, Shoram, and Zonta took off into the breaking waves and headed out toward the far rocks. Soon they disappeared in the water.

"Why don't you stay here with your sketchbook?" Jaxon said to Allie. "I'll be back."

"But where are you going?" Allie asked.

"It's a surprise. You'll see!" he said brightly. With that, Jaxon hopped up on the magic log and was gone. Allie found a nice spot in the sunshine near one of the tide pools and began to draw the purple and orange sea stars that she saw in the water. As she looked closely, she saw some enormous purple-red sea urchins. When all their spines were erect, each one was as big as Jaxon's soccer ball.

I've never seen those before. They're huge, she thought. *I'll draw a picture so I can ask Dad about them.* She took up her purple and red colored pencils and began outlining the sea urchins' dramatic shapes.

Just as Allie was finishing the drawing, Jaxon reappeared on the magic log carrying his soccer ball. "We can teach the dragons to play soccer!" he said, triumphantly holding his ball high in the air.

"What a great idea!" Allie said. "It's good and flat right here, and the sand is packed hard. This is going to be great! I bet the dragons will love soccer!"

Allie and Jaxon had to wait quite a while for all three dragons to come back, but they kept busy finding logs to use for goalposts. At last Zonta emerged from the water, smiling happily, a sizable stack of fish between his teeth. Zonta placed his catch in a shady pool. "I'm taking these home later," he said to the children.

"Good idea," said Allie.

Shoram and Shyla soon appeared, too, with satisfied smiles on their faces. It had been a good breakfast, indeed. The dragons were thinking about how nice it would be to stretch out in the sun for a nap.

"Who wants to learn a new game?" said Jaxon.

Suddenly all ears perked up. Shoram trumpeted, Shyla swished her tail, and Zonta hopped about excitedly. Niji squeaked. "We do!"

"We're going to play soccer. It's a special kind of soccer called dragon soccer," Jaxon explained. "We can use my soccer ball." He glanced at Zonta. "My Dad fixed the hole from before." Zonta looked at the sand.

"Anyway," said Jaxon, "we're going to make two teams, and we can use this huge flat place in the sand for our field. See those two sets of logs at each end of the field?" He gestured with the ball. The dragons looked and nodded.

Jaxon continued, "One team tries to kick the ball between those two logs over there to score a point, and the other team tries to stop them from making the score. Each side wants to get the ball to the opposite goal. Here, Allie and I can show you."

The dragons watched while Jaxon and Allie kicked the ball up and down the field. "Do you get it?" Jaxon asked hopefully. Shoram and Zonta nodded yes. Shyla wasn't so sure.

"Oh, and one important thing," Jaxon added. "You can kick the ball with your back feet and hit it with your tail, but you can't pick it up with your front feet or scoop it up with your wings. Unless you're the goalie guarding the two posts. Then you can use everything you've got—wings, tails, and feet." Shyla liked the idea of hitting the ball with her tail. And she thought being a goalie sounded like fun.

They formed two teams. Team One included Shyla, Allie, and Zonta. Jaxon and Shoram were Team Two. They practiced until the dragons learned how to kick the ball and score a goal with their tails. The first time Shoram tried a kick, he ended up on his back in the sand, rubbery spikes sticking up every which way. Jaxon doubled over laughing.

Things changed once it was Shoram's turn to be a goalie. Jaxon knew he could score and made a solid kick, but the dragon's wide wings took care of the ball in one lightning move. Now it was Shoram's turn to laugh.

Before long they were all ready to start a game. Team One formed a huddle. "Shyla, you be the goalie," said Allie. "You're a natural. Zonta and I can be the forwards."

Jaxon and Shoram gave each other an enthusiastic high five. They were sure they were going to win. Though outnumbered, the two fellows were big and strong, and Shoram was a quick study.

"Get ready to lose!" Jaxon yelled at Team One. Allie ignored him, but Shyla whipped her tail around as a reminder that she had some skills Jaxon couldn't match. Zonta was on his best behavior with Jaxon. He didn't want to lose any of his new friends, or his fishing partners, either.

Team One started, Allie and Zonta moving the ball quickly down the beach. Zonta learned right away that he had to kick gently because he was so much stronger than Allie. He growled when Jaxon stole the ball in a feint and started it back in the other direction, passing it back and forth with Shoram. Before they knew it, Team Two had the ball down at the other end, and Shoram hit it with his tail. The ball flew right between Shyla's legs. A goal!

"Yes!" yelled Jaxon. Shoram trumpeted, and Team One looked confused, but not for long.

Back to the center with the ball. Zonta and Allie now had the ball and were doing a great job of passing it back and forth, when Jaxon took it away again. Zonta hopped backward, hooked the ball with his tail, and passed it to Allie, who took a header and sent it down the field toward their goal. Then Shoram appeared out of nowhere and, having seen Allie hit the ball with her head, stuck his big blue head out to take another header. Only this time the ball landed on the big red spike right at the top of his neck. *Hissssss . . .* The ball fell limply to the ground.

"Oh no!" shouted Jaxon. "Not again! Shoram, why didn't you watch what you were doing?"

Shoram looked puzzled. "I did watch. I did exactly what Allie just did!"

"You put a hole in my best soccer ball with your big red spike, man!" Jaxon yelled back angrily. "Stupid dragon," he muttered.

Shoram was beginning to get angry, too. He started huffing and puffing and pawing at the sand. Allie and the other dragons came running.

"Chill out, Jaxon!" said Allie. "We can fix your ball when we get back to Seattle. We'll find something else to use for dragon soccer."

"I know," volunteered Zonta. "There are some sea urchins in the tide pool over there. We can use one of those."

"No way," Shyla interrupted. "Those are alive. If we used one of them as a ball we'd kill it. And Mom might toast our tails! Besides, I put those there. I brought those up from the deep water because they're so pretty. But I have another idea."

Shoram looked at his sister with admiration. She was almost as good as their mother at solving problems, and he hoped she could get him out of trouble with his friend.

"Why don't we try and seal the hole in the ball by breathing a little fire on it? If we do it just right we can blow it up with the first breath, then seal the hole with fire on the second breath before the air can escape."

"That's a great idea!" cried Allie.

Jaxon looked doubtful, but he didn't want to quit the game. They helped Shyla find two rocks to hold the ball. When she got it in just the right position, she took a deep breath and blew.

"Look, it's puffing up!" shouted Allie over the noise. Then they watched Shyla let out a delicate stream of fire right at the hole. Sure enough, the hole was sealed. The ball was as good as new. Well, almost. The newly repaired place was melted a little unevenly, creating a ragged edge. But everyone agreed the ball was just fine for dragon soccer.

Back to the game they went. The three dragons now knew they shouldn't try to hit the ball with their heads. Play continued fast and furious, back and forth, back and forth. Finally Zonta and Allie scored a goal. Now the score was one to one. Shyla cheered by swishing her tail in the air, and Zonta jumped up and down until the ground shook.

Jaxon and Shoram now had the ball. Fast and strong, the two were driving the ball toward their goal. They were so absorbed in the game that they didn't hear a high whistling sound. When he saw that the goal was clear, Jaxon kicked the ball hard and straight in.

"Score!" he yelled. But before the word was out of his mouth, the ball bounced back out! Allie and Zonta tried to get the ball, but Jaxon held on to it and kicked it into the goal again. Once again it bounced back.

"Hey, what's going on?" he yelled.

"Where's Shyla?" shouted Allie. "Why isn't she defending the goal?" Suddenly they heard a high-pitched giggle. Meanwhile Shoram got the ball. He tried to drive the ball into the goal with his tail. Like Jaxon's kicks, it should have gone straight in, but instead it bounced out.

"What gives?" yelled Jaxon. He really wanted to score that goal. He was getting frustrated.

By now the giggling was much louder and had turned into outrageous laughter. Suddenly, Shoram knew what was going on. "Stop it, Shyla!" he trumpeted. "You'd better whistle a low C before I jump on you!"

"But you don't know where I am," Shyla's voice teased from up above them. Shyla had made herself invisible. An invisible goalie! Jaxon and Allie burst into gales of laughter. Shoram, not about to let his sister get the better of him, started jumping and flapping around, trying to find her. Shyla giggled, easily evading him.

"Look out, Jaxon! Shoram's apt to flip over and land on you," Allie yelled, then started laughing as Jaxon dodged his teammate. Shoram flapped, flipped over, tripped, whistled, and thumped his tail on the sand in vexation, but Shyla would not appear. Soon the two children were doubled over in laughter, and Zonta was guffawing right along. At that moment, Shyla whistled low C and *poof!* There she was again: orchid-pink, tail swishing, with a droll look on her face.

Phew! What a game! After another round of play, they all agreed it was time to stop and rest. The dragons decided that dragon soccer was definitely a great game and they should play it again. Zonta was in a much happier state than when he arrived that morning. And Allie—well, she was worn out trying to keep up with the dragons, but her cheeks were rosy and her eyes were shining.

Just then sharp-eyed Shyla noticed a dark blot in the sky to the south. "What's that?" She pointed, and everyone looked up.

"It's my dad," muttered Zonta. "I hope he doesn't ruin everything."

The children didn't know what to say. They liked Zonta, but his father Zorg was another matter. Fortunately the spot grew no larger, and gradually everyone began to relax again.

Trying to recapture his happy mood, Zonta nodded toward the north end of the beach. "What's that funny-looking shape over there?" he asked. "I've never gone that far north before."

Shoram followed his gaze. "Oh, it's just another set of sea stacks with arches and caves," he replied. "But I've heard the magic is really, really strong down there, especially when the fog is in."

Jaxon and Allie glanced down the beach. "We've got our own name for that one. We call it the Witch's House 'cause it looks all crooked and spooky."

"Let's go down there tomorrow," suggested Shyla. "I'm not ready for any more adventure today." But this talk of magic had gotten her thinking. "You know, we could go find the magic pool now. It's close by, and maybe it would let Zonta change color. Would you like that, Zonta?"

"You bet!" cried Zonta. "Which way is it?"

Shoram wasn't so sure about this. He hadn't quite made up his mind yet to be friends with Zonta, but he didn't say anything. Jaxon and Allie were certain they didn't want to change color, but they sure wanted to watch it happen.

Once they had located the pool, they all began digging vigorously. Soon the beautiful silvery water began to flow into the hole.

"What do I have to do?" asked Zonta, suddenly feeling a bit queasy.

"The pool lets you change colors, especially if you're a kind and helpful dragon to others, and not selfish," said Shyla. Shoram stuck in his front leg to demonstrate, and thought *green*. He pulled his leg back out to show the others. It was green! Zonta was amazed. He wanted to be a bright shimmery color like the Shi Shi dragons instead of his family's dull gray-green.

Zonta jumped into the pool. He heard a rumbling and grumbling sound as the water churned around him.

"So, you want to change color, then?" the pool asked.

"Yes, please," replied Zonta with his best manners.

"Well, it may be possible. You used to behave quite badly, rather like your father. Now it seems you are willing to catch fish to share with your family. Very good. Still, you do not respect all the other animal life around you. Greater kindness is in order. But we'll see what we can do." And with that the water began to bubble and burble, and Zonta could feel his skin beginning to tickle and prickle.

"Oh my gosh!" Zonta exclaimed as he climbed out of the pool. His former gray-green had almost completely faded away, and a soft orange color shone through from underneath.

"Zonta, you're beautiful!" exclaimed Shyla. Allie and Jaxon clapped, and Shoram tried to blow a steam ring like his mother's, but he couldn't quite do it. Zonta hopped up and down in his new scales.

"The three of you together look like the sunset on the beach," exclaimed Allie. "Blue, orchid, and soft orange." She rummaged for her pencils to see if she had a good color to draw Zonta's new look. But Jaxon looked at the western horizon and realized that the sun really was almost setting. They'd spent the whole day playing and having fun, and now it was time to go.

The silvery water of the magic pool disappeared back into the sand. All the dragons began working together to fill the hole back in. Zonta collected his fish, and they all watched their newly beautiful orange friend take off to return to his home beach. "See you tomorrow, I hope!" Zonta called out as he flew into the distance.

Jaxon picked up his soccer ball. "See you tomorrow!" he called to Shoram and Shyla. Allie waved farewell as they both hopped up onto the magic log.

"I'm so glad we got to see the dragons again," said Allie as they walked back to camp. "It makes me feel all happy."

Jaxon nodded in agreement. "Yeah, it was so cool. Even if Shoram did put a hole in my soccer ball." He ran his finger over the repaired spot. "My friends would never believe me if I told them this ball was punctured by a dragon spike!"

"Or that it was repaired with dragon fire!" added Allie.

eleven ZORG'S TRUE COLORS

The fog was thick on the beach when the dragons awoke. Tendrils of mist swirled in all directions. In some places it was so thick they couldn't see 10 feet in front of them. In other places it thinned out to wispy steam that curled in and out of the trees and rocks. Then it looked like the steam that arose from the water when the dragons were fishing. Shalini loved watching her delicate steam rings blend and disappear in the drifts of mist and fog.

Over on Stinky Fish Beach Zorg awoke with a strange feeling in his heart. Ever since he had been struck in his soft spot, he had felt different. He wasn't much inclined to steal fish or harass the Shi Shi dragons. But his grumpy manner hadn't changed. Zorg still chased the gulls and other creatures, and he didn't want to make the effort to fish for himself. Mostly he still hung around near his cave, snoozing in the sun or scratching his gray-green scales. Zonta did most of the fishing now, and Zorgina was quietly pleased about her son's delicate new orange scales.

This morning Zorg was feeling rather restless. Something was going to happen, he was sure, but he didn't know what. And that made him nervous. Then from out of nowhere he felt the old fish-stealing urge returning. The temptation was familiar and exciting, like seeing an old friend. "Let's go over to Shi Shi and get some fish!" he called out to Zonta.

"I don't think so, Dad," Zonta replied, looking down at his new colors. "I'm not stealing fish anymore. I want to get rid of the rest of these gray-green scales."

"Suit yourself," Zorg retorted, then took off into the fog.

Meanwhile Shoram and Shyla woke and stretched their necks. "Whad'ya think?" Shoram yawned. "Should we go down to the Witch's House today?"

"Sure," Shyla said, peering out into the fog. "But what about Zonta and our human friends? Don't you want to wait for them?"

"Oh, it's still really early. We can go down and check it out, then come back here for some breakfast. Then we can all go back to the Witch's House together."

"Okay," said Shyla, gliding out of her cave. She swished her tail and took off into the fog. "Last one there is a round raccoon!"

Not to be outflown, Shoram quickly took to the air. As they raced down the beach they did loops in the air, stirring up the fog with their tails and creating dramatic columns of fog that rose and arched in the air above the beach. Luckily for the two dragons, the fog lifted a bit so they saw the Witch's House before they crashed into it. Shlya coasted in gently, but Shoram overshot his landing and had to scramble onto the far side of the stack, nearly toppling over into the sand below. His sister smothered a giggle. Below them was an eerie patch of fog, swirling in beautiful patterns over the sand just where the waves broke on the shore.

"Shoram, look at that fog," said Shyla. "There's something funny about it. Let's go take a look." And she lifted off.

Down the young dragons flew, landing near the swirling patch of mist. Tendrils of moisture spun out and dissolved. New ones formed and disappeared. It was as if there were a center to this fog. "Let's go inside," Shyla urged, sticking her head into the swirls. Shoram wasn't so sure. As her head penetrated the fog, Shyla heard a deep, broad voice.

"What do you wish, young dragon miss?" Startled, Shyla pulled back a little.

"Who are you?" asked Shyla. Then she stopped. What she'd said didn't sound very friendly, and she wanted to keep the golden tip on her tail.

"I am the magic fog that helps dragons open their hearts and change if they wish to do so," the mist replied. "You must respect my power. But you seem to be a kind young dragon, so be on your way. Surely you have no need of me." And with that, the fog swirled into a tight column and disappeared down into the sand.

Shyla and Shoram peered closely at the sand, speechless. After a minute Shyla said, "See those silver flecks? They're sort of like the ones in the magic pool near our caves. Do you suppose this is another magic pool?"

Shoram nodded. "C'mon! Let's go back and tell the others!" He began flapping and took to the air.

"Wait for me!" Shyla called. She flew above Shoram, teasing by occasionally swooping down on him and threatening to knock him off balance. He retaliated by zooming above her and doing loops around her. Shyla dove under Shoram, and soon the two were laughing so hard while doing loops and barrel rolls around each other that they almost crashed onto the beach. They decided after that to be a little more careful. They knew what their father would have to say about dragons who can't stay in the air.

They skidded to a landing just as Shalini came out of her cave. "What have you two been up to so early in the morning?" she asked.

Poised on Shalini's forehead, Niji scolded them: *Squeak, squeak, squeak-a-squeak!* "Why didn't you take me with you?"

"We think we've found another magic pool down by the Witch's House," Shyla said breathlessly. "It's got lots of magic mist above it."

"Is that so?" said Shalini. She was quiet for a moment. "Let me think," she mused. "I do seem to remember something about a magic pool down there. It was a very old and sage pool, even when I was young. It had a reputation for being able to help you change if you really wanted to." The young ones gazed at their mother. Shyla wondered if she would ever know as much as her mother did, or be as wise.

Suddenly Niji gave a loud squeak. They looked up and saw a menacing black dot in the sky, approaching rapidly.

"I think Zorg's coming," said Shalini. "Everyone back into their caves!"

"I've got an idea," whispered Shoram to Shyla. "Let's have some fun with him." So he and Shyla stayed behind as Zorg approached them on the beach. The young blue and red dragon stepped forward as Zorg landed near the fish storage pool.

"You're wasting your time, Zorg," Shoram said. "We haven't gone fishing yet today so there aren't even any fish to steal." Zorg snarled.

"But there's a big pool of fish down at the other end of the beach," Shoram continued. "They're trapped in a pool by the outgoing tide. Why don't you come down there with us? You can have all the fish you want."

Zorg was suspicious to his very bones. Why was this Shi Shi dragon being so friendly? And in spite of the tenderness of his soft spot, he was still in a grumpy mood. Most of all he was hungry, really ravenous. The fish Zonta had brought home yesterday had barely whetted his appetite. He wheeled around and growled.

"All right! Show me where these fish are. But there'd better not be any tricks!" He snarled once again, much louder, but Shoram stood his ground.

Off they flew, Shoram leading the way with Niji on his back, followed by Shyla and

Zorg. When they got to the Witch's House they all landed on the roof. It was rather crowded, and Zorg was perched at the very edge of the rock.

"So, where are all these fish?" Zorg growled suspiciously.

Shyla looked down and saw that the mystical fog had reappeared, just in time. She pointed with her tail to the swirling column. Within it, tendrils of fog began to form the shapes of silvery fish swimming about. They moved in and out, shimmering in the shafts of sunlight that occasionally broke through the mist.

Zorg looked at her suspiciously. "Okay, if there's so many fish, why don't you go in first!" He swung his massive head back and forth menacingly.

"Well," Shyla replied, "because you'd just steal them from us. Besides, I'm not hungry. We already had breakfast." It was only a small fib, and she really wasn't hungry.

"They're easy to catch," she urged. "Just jump in the pool and grab some."

Zorg's hunger was stronger than his distrust. Down he jumped into the patch of magic mist. It engulfed him almost completely. Soon only his head and the smallest tip of his tail were showing against the dark sand. But that sand was no longer solid! It had opened out into a pool of water. Now the shapes that had seemed to be fish were only curls of fog and ripples of water that dissolved when Zorg tried to catch them.

"*Aargh!*" Zorg growled, twisting and lunging at the fish shapes, trying to stay afloat in the pool. The big dragon had never been a good swimmer—that was the main reason he didn't like fishing. Suddenly Zorg forgot about food. He just wanted out of the water. As he struggled, the sand began to close in around him. From underneath it grabbed his tail and legs, then his wings. Zorg sank until only his head was free. He growled, he roared, he whined, but he was thoroughly stuck! And the magic mist continued swirling about the big dragon's head.

"Zorg!" The voice of the pool was deep and warm. Zorg stopped struggling to listen. "After those beautiful red rocks struck your soft spot, you felt a change in yourself. Isn't that so?"

"Well, I guess so . . ." said the dragon hesitantly.

"And what has happened?"

Zorg thought for a moment. It was true that lately he just wasn't interested in scaring seagulls—one of his favorite pastimes! He hadn't blown a burst of fire at the birds in quite a while. *Hmm,* what else? He hadn't gone out stealing fish! Not until just this morning, anyway. The gray-green dragon shook his head and muttered to himself. The young dragons watched, keeping their distance. They didn't want to get scorched if Zorg's mood suddenly changed.

The morning sun was now peeking through the thick fog. Soon the mist had evaporated and there was Zorg, still trapped in the sand. The more he struggled, the more he realized he was hopelessly stuck.

Back at the south end of the beach, Shalini and Shiran were getting ready to go fishing for breakfast when they noticed something in the fog. A faintly orange dragon—a young one—was approaching.

"Who in the world is that?" wondered Shiran. As the young dragon landed, they recognized him.

"Why, it's Zonta!" exclaimed Shalini.

Zonta hopped about. "Hi. Where's Shoram? And Shyla?"

"They've gone down to the other end of the beach, to the Witch's House. By the way, your dad was out here earlier, down that way." Shalini looked around. "But I don't see him just now."

This worried Zonta. He knew his dad might be planning to steal fish, and he figured Shoram and Shyla might try to stop him. And that wouldn't be pretty! *I'd better check out the Witch's House,* he thought.

"Thanks. Gotta go!" said Zonta, and in a flash he was an orange blur in the air.

Just then Jaxon and Allie appeared on the magic log.

"My, it's a busy beach today!" said Shalini as the two children bounded toward her.

"Where are Shyla and Shoram?" asked Jaxon, tossing his soccer ball around.

Shalini repeated what she had just told Zonta. "He left in quite a hurry. I was surprised to see he's acquired some orange scales!" Shalini sounded pleased.

"They left without us," complained Allie. "How are we ever going to get all the way down there by ourselves?"

"You could walk," suggested Shiran. The great dragon was accustomed to covering the entire beach in just a few minutes and not many steps.

"But that will take us forever—and we wanted everybody to explore the Witch's House together!" Allie tried not to whine, but Shalini heard the disappointment in her voice.

"Perhaps we can take you down there. Would you care to ride on our backs?" said the mother dragon with a smile.

The children had been hoping for just such an invitation. Quickly they climbed Shiran and Shalini's outstretched necks and made their way up onto the backs of the great dragons. Jaxon held tightly onto the pink spike in front of him with one hand, hugging his soccer ball to his chest with the other. Jaxon and Allie were now used to balancing on the flying dragons, and it wasn't long before they spotted their friends gathered on the beach near the Witch's House. As they landed, they saw, in the center of the young dragons' circle, a frustrated Zorg stuck in the sand and squirming.

"What's all this?" asked Shalini. Shoram, Shyla, and Niji explained, while Zorg just bellowed. Poor Zonta was at a loss. He wanted to help his father, but how?

Shiran surveyed the scene and said, "It appears this is the next step in Zorg's change of heart. First he took those blows to his soft spot with the red heart rocks.

But now he must want to change his ways before the sand will let him go." He paused and added, "He's in good hands."

The great dragon turned to Zonta. "You mustn't worry for your father. The sand will not harm him."

Shiran gestured to Shalini, and the two headed toward the waves for their day's fishing.

As the morning passed, the fog burned off until the beach was bright with sunshine. Even so, occasional wisps of mist curled in and out of the caves and crevices at the base of the Witch's House. The children and dragons explored caves filled with pools and creatures. As the sun moved across the sky, the day grew hotter. The young dragons and children relished the cool, seaweed-covered walls as they rested in the shade. Every so often they checked on Zorg, who only glared at them.

"His head looks kind of like a green rock," observed Jaxon. He said to Zonta, "I think your dad might be getting a sunburn. Should we cover him with some seaweed to cool him off?"

"I'll go get some!" said Zonta, grateful to his human friend for the idea. He hurried off to the shallow water to gather some fresh kelp. With Jaxon and Allie's help, he covered his father's neck and the top of his head with cool seaweed. Zorg was surprised and touched to be getting this kind of attention. Why were they doing this? He began feeling a pulsing throb in his chest, just around his heart. It was the same feeling he'd noticed after being hit in his soft spot.

"How about some dragon soccer?" asked Jaxon.

"Great!" shouted Shoram and Shyla together. "We can play on that flat part of the beach over there." They set about fixing up the goalposts and marking out the playing field.

"Niji, how about you being the referee?" asked Jaxon. Niji thought that would be fun, so they began to teach him the rules of the game.

The teams were the same as before: Jaxon and Shoram played against Allie, Shyla, and Zonta. "And no becoming invisible, Shyla. It's not fair," warned Shoram. Shyla looked the other way and swished her tail slightly.

The play was fast and furious. Soon each team had scored two goals. Niji was getting a workout, flying back and forth and squeaking loudly. He kept getting the rules mixed up, calling fouls when there weren't any, not calling fouls when they occurred, giving the ball to the wrong team. At last Shyla said, gently so as not to hurt his feelings, "Niji, we love your enthusiasm, but how about you taking a break for a while? You can watch the game from up in that tall fir tree, okay?"

Tired and relieved, Niji perched on Shyla's head to catch his breath. When he had recovered his strength a bit, Niji flew up into the fir tree where he could watch the game from above. But as tired as he was, the little dragon couldn't stop himself from giving a running commentary, squeaking loudly each time someone stole the ball.

Zorg had finally quit struggling in the sand. Without

quite realizing it, he had become interested in watching the young ones at their game. He'd never known Zonta to play with other dragons before. To Zorg's surprise, his heart warmed. Yes, he liked seeing his son having a good time with friends.

Now it was Zonta's turn to be goalie. He was thrilled to realize that he could protect the entire goal with his out-stretched wings. Shoram had the ball and was rapidly approaching. He flicked it with his tail and sent it sailing. But Zonta stuck his wing in the air and caught the ball just in time!

"Great going, Zonta!" shouted Jaxon sportingly. He was on the opposite team, but a good save was a good save! Off to the side, Zorg began following Zonta's every move to protect the goal. Again Zorg felt a familiar warmth in his chest. And there was something else, too. He felt proud of his son.

As Zonta put the ball back in play, Jaxon grabbed it and passed it to Shoram, who maneuvered the ball behind him with his tail and returned it to Jaxon. One hard kick, and the ball neared the goal. Zonta's attention wavered just for a moment, and the ball slipped under his wing to score. "Hurray!" shouted Shoram, giving Jaxon a high five with his huge front foot.

"Let's take a break," said Allie. "I'm getting tired, aren't you, Shyla?" The sun was now high in the sky. Her friend nodded, and they all ran out to cool off in the waves.

Zorg watched the young ones with a wistful whimper. The seaweed on his neck was no longer cool. It had dried into a stiff, scratchy blanket. As he looked out from under the fronds over his horns at the children and dragons, his heart softened a little more. Suddenly Zorg shouted out to all of them.

"I'm sorry for all the trouble I've caused you!" he called. The dragons and children stopped their splashing, astonished. They walked up out of the water to listen, as Zorg continued speaking through his hat of dried seaweed.

"And I'm sorry I wasted so much fish," he said. "I'm not going to do that anymore. And no more chasing seagulls or deer, either. I don't want them to be scared of me."

They all looked at Zonta. He was doing his best to act as though nothing unusual was happening. But hearing these words from his father, Zonta felt like dancing.

Suddenly Niji, still keeping watch in the fir tree, flew down and began squeaking excitedly. "There's someone coming!" Another dragon was flying down the beach toward the group.

"Who can it be?" wondered Shyla aloud.

Zonta recognized the flight pattern. "It's my mom," he said quietly. In a few minutes Zorgina landed on the beach next to them and looked at everyone. Her eyes were large and sad. She went to her husband.

"Oh Zorg, what have you gotten yourself into now?" she asked. Zorgina was frowning, but her voice was gentle. Zorg responded with a muffled growl. His voice sounded crackly. Shyla stepped closer to explain what had happened. She spoke only about the events of the day, not mentioning all the mean things Zorg had done to them throughout the summer.

Zorgina was a kindhearted dragon. Living on the land with grumpy Zorg had made her sad and quiet. But she could see that her husband was extremely thirsty. Zorgina went over to a small stream nearby, scooped up some water with her wing, and offered it to Zorg, who drank it gratefully.

Zorgina sat down beside Zorg's head. She removed the dried seaweed from his neck and poured water over his scorched back. She fanned his face with her wing to cool him off. Zorg closed his eyes as his heart softened even more.

And then something happened in Zorg's tired mind. He began to remember old times, when his family had been happy living in their peaceful kingdom under the sea. Zorg remembered how he had been kind to others in those days, and how they had been kind to him. He remembered how proud he had been to be a good father to little Zonta and a good husband to Zorgina. He had felt grateful in those days for the help and support his fellow dragons had given them. Remembering these things, Zorg wished he could feel that way again.

To Zorgina he said softly, "I'm sorry for all the hard times I've given you. I want things to be as they were before. I still remember how to be kind, and I'm willing to catch our own fish. I want to be friendly to the Shi Shi dragons, the way they've befriended Zonta. I don't want to waste food anymore . . ." Zorg went on, listing all the ways he would change. Zorgina's eyes lit up and she purred gently.

Suddenly, in the midst of the heat, a cloud of mist began to swirl about Zorg's head. Dragons and children stared in astonishment for several minutes, as the mist engulfed Zorg and kept swirling. Now and then they could see that Zorg's dull gray-green color seemed to be changing, as glimmers of gold flashed through the mist. They heard strange slurping noises, as if water were mixing with the sand in which Zorg was trapped. Suddenly they saw a wing poking out of the fog. And then another. The wings were a beautiful, shimmery green edged in luminous gold. Then there was a loud *shlurrrrp!* as Zorg heaved himself out of the wet sand onto the beach.

"Dad, you're fabulous!" Zonta gasped. Before them stood a soft green Zorg, his scales glistening gold in the sunlight. Then Zonta felt his own skin prickling a little, and he turned to look down his back. The old gray-green had completely disappeared. His skin and scales were now a bright deep orange. Zonta turned to show his mother.

"Mom! Look what's happened to you!" he cried, gazing at Zorgina in delight.

Zorgina, too, had been engulfed by the magic mist when it first appeared. But they had all been so intent on watching Zorg that no one had noticed Zorgina turning a brilliant ruby red!

The Shi Shi dragons and the children stared at the Zorg dragons, admiring their transformation. Then they heard the deep, warm voice of the mist.

"It is possible to accomplish great change in oneself," it said. "But you must desire it from within the deepest place in your heart." The group looked at each other and nodded in agreement.

The mist spoke again. "Zorg, your wife and son have shown you the way. And your heart has opened as well. Follow that way, follow your heart, and again you will become the mighty dragon you were long ago. I have not changed you. In fact, I have only restored your true colors." With those words, the mist swept and swirled into a tight column and disappeared into the sand. Zorg stood motionless, blinking in the bright sunshine.

The beach was silent except for the sound of the waves. Dragons and children stood amazed. The changing of colors had indeed been miraculous, but all of them knew that the real miracle was the changing of Zorg's heart. Each one of them had played a small role in this change. Now each one held that memory close. And in the deepest place in their hearts, they each felt glad about helping Zorg to reclaim his true colors as he remembered what he had known long ago when he lived under the sea.

"Wow," Shoram finally said. He didn't need to trumpet. "Fantastic day, huh? We should celebrate!"

"Yes," said Shyla. "Let's go back to the point. We can go fishing and have a party! Allie, hop on my back. I promise I won't do any loops!"

Before Shoram could make Jaxon the same offer, Zonta had stepped up. With a grin, Jaxon swung up onto Zonta's warm orange neck.

So, with Jaxon and Allie on board and Niji riding on Shyla's back, one great spike in front of Allie, the dragons took off for the point with Zorgina in the lead. Riderless, Shoram decided to do loops around the whole group, until they were half dizzy from watching him.

They landed near the caves of the Shi Shi dragons just as Shiran and Shalini appeared. They'd fished all morning and then enjoyed an afternoon nap, unaware of all that had happened at the other end of the beach. Seeing the brightly colored Zorgs, Shalini said, "Ah! I see the magic mist has helped complete the change. You all look radiant!" She arched her neck toward Zorgina, and the two mother dragons blew gentle steam rings, which twined and twirled in the air above their heads.

The dragons soon agreed to go on a joint outing to catch fish for the party. Jaxon and Allie wanted to stay, but they knew their parents were expecting them back for dinner around the campfire. *And tomorrow we'll be heading back to Seattle!* Allie thought sadly. The children hugged each dragon around the neck. They even hugged Zorg, who didn't growl or snarl in the least.

"We'll back next summer for sure," said Allie, giving Shyla and Niji an extra squeeze.

"And maybe for a weekend in September," added Jaxon, giving Shoram one last big hug. Reluctantly, Allie and Jaxon headed for the magic log.

"You'll always be welcome on Shi Shi," the dragons called as they waved goodbye.

twelve THE SKY DRAGON

That night on Shi Shi, all the dragons feasted on fish. In his exuberance, Zorg had caught more than anyone! The dragons made a fire by breathing on a pile of wood they had collected. Then they lay back on the beach, warming themselves. As the fire burned down to coals, they watched the stars come out.

Suddenly the sky brightened in the north. An arc appeared low across the sky, with flashes of light dancing and wavering every so often.

"It's the breathing of the Sky Dragon," whispered Shalini. "She appears and becomes visible when all's right with the world, when dragons are at peace with one another."

As they watched, a magnificent band of light began to

form across the heavens. It reached from the trees behind the Witch's House across the sky above them, and ended in the water beyond Lookout Rock. The light shimmered and shone in waves that rippled and undulated. As they watched, they saw that the color of every dragon among them was also present in the sky, from Shyla's orchid to Zorgina's new soft ruby, even to the brilliant green that still showed at the tip of Shoram's nose.

The dragons were speechless at the beauty above them. Only Shiran and Shalini had seen this before. Humans called it the northern lights, but the elder Shi Shi dragons knew it was the fire of the Sky Dragon, who was pleased with Zorg's transformation and the peace among the dragons this evening. Together they watched the sky for a long time, as one by one they gently drifted off to sleep.

Back at camp Allie snuggled under Dad's arm, and Jaxon and Mom sat close together, leaning against their favorite log. They, too, were watching the haze of colored lights dancing across the night sky as the campfire embers glowed.

"Amazing luck, this great view of the northern lights," Dad said. "I've never seen them before."

"Look Mom, there's Draco, right next to the band of light!" Jaxon exclaimed, pointing. "That's the dragon constellation."

"Where'd you learn so much about dragons?" Mom asked. Jaxon and Allie smiled.

The family gazed up at Draco. For a moment it did indeed look as though Draco was breathing out a stream of light. What a day it had been. The children closed their eyes, touched in the deepest places in their hearts. It seemed to them both as if their hearts were filled with color and light. And they drifted off to sleep in a deep, contented pink mist, with blue-green and golden wishes for the happiness of the dragons, and with orange and ruby-red memories of the magic of Shi Shi Beach.

THE WILD AND BEAUTIFUL COAST
OF THE PACIFIC NORTHWEST

Shi Shi Beach (pronounced *shy-shy*) is one of the many beautiful beaches of the Pacific Northwest Coast. From British Columbia to southern Oregon, rocky headlands, as well as secluded coves and beaches, create the perfect habitats for many different sea animals and plants.

The weather gives this land its beauty. Winter storms crash against rocky headlands, slowly carving out sea caves and arches. These storms also form the sea stacks, such as the magnificent Point of the Arches at the south end of Shi Shi Beach. Sea stacks are rounded rock formations found offshore. Perhaps early European settlers called them "stacks" because they looked like large haystacks from a distance. The winter storms also bring driftwood logs of all sizes onto the beaches. Summer campers like Jaxon and Allie's family often use these interesting pieces of wood to build campsites.

In the Forest

The thick, rich forests of the Pacific Northwest, with their tall Douglas firs, western red cedars, hemlocks, and Sitka spruce, come right down to the edge of the beach. These towering trees, many of which cling to the edges of cliffs adjoining the beaches, reach their tremendous sizes due to the nourishing rains. Fog often shrouds the coastline in mystery. To get to Shi Shi Beach, you have to walk through several miles of this deep forest.

The forest is home to many animals, such as blacktail deer, raccoons, squirrels, and chipmunks. All of them venture out onto the beach to feed. Watch out for raccoons and chipmunks that love to raid campsites for food! And the misty, foggy forest is perfect for the five- to seven-inch banana slugs that slime their way across the forest floor.

On the Beach

On the beaches you'll see gulls looking for food, mewing loudly as they chase each other. Gulls and other seabirds build their nests on the rocky ledges of the sea stacks. Delicate sandpipers, small birds with long legs, scurry along the water's edge feeding on little creatures left behind by the outgoing tide. Black oystercatchers with bright red bills pick mussels and other food from the rocks at low tide. Occasionally you may see an eagle flying overhead or perching on a tree as it seeks fish or other prey.

In the Tide Pools

The deep tide pools that exist between the high and low tides on the rocky shores of the coast are teeming with all kinds of sea life. Each tide pool is a small, unique wilderness, a world of its own. Purple and orange sea stars cling to the rocks. (Sea stars were once called "starfish," but they're actually not fish at all.) Big blue-green sea anemones, crabs (including hermit crabs who live in empty snail shells), mussels, barnacles, limpets, chitons, periwinkle snails, dog whelks, sea slugs, sea cucumbers, and small fish are only some of the many, many animals that live in the tide pools. Sometimes these creatures hide on the undersides of rocks. At other times they stay sheltered by seaweed so they won't dry out in the sun. The seaweed itself comes in all sizes, shapes, and colors—red, orange, brown, shimmering purple, gold, and green—like a rainbow in the sea.

Below the Low Tide Line
Beneath the low tide line is another wilderness. Big forests of bull kelp just off shore are home to many kinds of fish. Living here also are the big burgundy sea urchins that the dragon Shyla loves so much. Sea urchins, as well as crabs, are food for sea otters living in the kelp forests. There are so many kinds of fish in the Pacific Northwest waters that we can't name them all! But of course, the favorite of dragons and people (and resident orca whales) are the salmon. Adult salmon swim through these waters in the summer and fall months on their way back to their home rivers to spawn.

Seals and sea lions play in the water here. They dive down to feed on fish and marine animals, then climb ashore on rocky ledges or small beaches to warm themselves in the sun. Some seals will approach swimmers or kayaks (and perhaps even dragons!) simply because they're curious.

What About the Dragons?

You've read about just a few of the many animals, plants, and other life you may see when you visit the outer coast of the Pacific Northwest. As you wander these extraordinary beaches, sea stacks, caves, and arches, there's no guarantee you'll meet the dragons who live under the sand in winter and in caves during the summer. Even seasoned explorers cannot say for sure when the dragons will appear. That's a mystery that belongs to those with scales and wings and the breath of fire.

Some Books About the Pacific Beaches and Tide Pools

There are many ways to learn more about the tide pools that Allie, Jaxon, and the dragons explored in this story. Start with the book *Tide Pools*, by Melissa Cole. You'll see some of the orange sea stars that Allie thought were so beautiful. Another good book with great pictures of creatures like the shy hermit crab is *Animals of the Sea and Shore*, by Ann Squire. You might also look for *Sea Critters* by Sylvia Earle, published by the National Geographic Society. This book has amazing pictures of sea life from the biggest whales to the delicate sea urchins that live near Shi Shi Beach.

Asian Dragons

Dragons are often seen in paintings and tapestries, but there aren't any photographs of these huge creatures so some people don't believe they exist. But they have existed for thousands of years in stories and legends in Asia, particularly in China and Japan.

The dragons of Asia are wise, beautiful, and powerful. They are the most noble of beasts, and often live near or under water. They are worshiped and honored in shrines that are built to them along the water's edge. In times of drought they are responsible for bringing rain to the parched land and saving the crops. But they can also be vain and can cause trouble, such as storms, if people do not follow their advice.

In both China and Japan it is thought that the emperor was descended from the dragon, and thus the royal robes are covered with beautiful, embroidered dragons. The dragon is the symbol of divine protection and ultimate good fortune. People honor dragons in festivals, with large paper dragons in parades, dragon boat races, dragon kites, and dragon decorations.

European Dragons

There are lots of stories from hundreds of years ago about dragons in all parts of Europe. Norse dragons were said to guard the graves of kings. In Germany and Britain, dragons were fierce fighters, and brave knights would have to slay a dragon in order to rescue a beautiful princess or recover stolen treasure. These dragons didn't have as much to do with water as the Asian dragons, and they weren't very friendly to humans.

Dragons of the Pacific Northwest

The dragons of the Pacific Northwest most closely resemble Asian dragons. They are kind and noble, wise and gentle (although they can be fierce), and they often live close to people, protecting them when necessary. They like to live near water, particularly along the rocky shores of the Pacific Ocean.

Pacific Northwest dragons have wings like European dragons. This may be the result of dragon migrations millions of years ago, when dragons were thought to exist all over the world. During a time when warm tropical forests existed everywhere, the northern regions of the earth were connected and Asian and European dragons had much contact with each other.

From this contact a breed of dragons arose who liked to live near water but also had wings to help them fly. As the planet cooled, they migrated south along coastlines and took up residence in various places along the Pacific Ocean.

Modern-day Dragons
Like their Asian relatives, Northwest dragons usually hibernate in the winter, either in underwater caves or dwellings or, as the Shi Shi dragons do, by burying themselves in the sand. In the summer they prefer to live in the cool caves and arches of the many sea stacks and rock

formations that abound on the Northwest coast. Also like their Asian cousins, the dragons of the Pacific Northwest do not hoard treasure. They seem to enjoy protecting the treasures of the natural world that surround them in their caves and tide pools.

Since their earliest roots are in the sea, Pacific Northwest dragons quickly adapted to eating fish, particularly salmon, which are plentiful during the summer months. For this reason they have become very adept at a particular method of fire-fishing. Sometimes they follow migrating schools of salmon, but more often they simply feed on the salmon they find in the waters close to their caves.

Dragon Families

Pacific Northwest dragons often live in family groups or tribes. When young dragons hatch from the egg, they're thought to be about 10 feet long, but no humans have ever seen a baby dragon. They grow quite rapidly in their early years and quickly reach a size that is about half that of an adult. From that point, however, their growth slows, and it takes about 150 years for them to reach full adult size.

The young stay with their parents until they are fully grown, which takes at least 200 years, and then they often choose to live nearby once they have formed their own families. They may leave for several years on adventures, and are known to travel to distant lands, particularly in Asia, to explore their heritage. A dragon can live for as long as 2,000 years!

Pacific Northwest dragons are large creatures as adults. They are about the size of a school bus, as much as 40 feet in length and 12 to 15 feet in height. Their wingspan is about 30 feet. As adults their scales are shimmery and shiny and reflect the light in beautiful ways. They can be found in all the colors of the rainbow.

The scales of adult dragons are very hard and cannot be penetrated by weapons of any sort. However, there is a small space located over the heart that the scales do not cover, and the skin is quite tender there. The otherwise tough and leathery skin on the rest of the body and wings is also quite thin and tender behind the ears and under the wings.

Legend or Reality?

The hardest question about dragons is deciding whether they really exist. Some people think they are just in our imagination. Others say that dragons do exist but are very secretive and have magic powers that keep humans from seeing them. What do you think?

Books About Dragons

Do you think it would be fun to take Niji home to your house like Allie wanted to? Here's a book that talks about doing just that, *Dragonology: Tracking and Taming Dragons*, by Ernest Drake. Not surprisingly there are no photographs of dragons, but there are plenty of good drawings and sketches of dragon footprints. Another way to learn about dragons is with the book *A Time of Golden Dragons*, by Song Nan Zhang and Hao Yu Zhang. You can read about how important dragons were in other lands and other cultures. And a third choice is the title *Mysterious Encounters —Dragons*, by Kelli Brucken.

ASIAN BRUSH PAINTING
SUMI-E

The Brush Dances and the Ink Sings

The Chinese have a saying, "The brush dances and the ink sings." This is a perfect description of a sumi-e painting (pronounced *soo-me-ay*). The artist is working to capture the essence or spirit or *qi* (pronounced *chi*) of her subject in the painting. When the painter is very familiar with her subject, for example her pet cat or dragon, her awareness of its essence will allow her to paint it very freely and simply. The brush will dance, the strokes will be lively and free, and the image will seem alive on the paper. Others will be drawn to looking at her cat (or dragon) painting because it is full of *qi*. A good sumi-e painter can make even rocks come alive!

Sumi-e means "ink picture" in Japanese. "Sumi" means ink and "e" means painting or picture. Similar styles of painting with brush and ink are often seen in other Asian countries, particularly China and Korea, and so this style of painting is now often referred to as Asian brush painting.

Sumi-e Paintings Are Alive

There are many folk stories that tell us about how thoroughly alive sumi-e paintings can be. One is about Sesshu, a Japanese master painter from the 14th century. As a boy, he displeased his teacher by drawing instead of studying his lessons. In punishment he was tied to a tree so that he would be forced to study. Instead, he drew such lifelike mice in the sand with his toe that they suddenly came to life and freed him by chewing through the ropes that held him!

The Early Days of Sumi-e

Ink painting began in China around 600 A.D. in the form of calligraphy, which means "beautiful writing." The brush strokes used to form Chinese characters are the basis of the brush strokes used in painting. Chinese characters are often pictorial representations of the meaning of the word, so it was a natural transition from writing characters to painting pictures. Japanese Zen Buddhist monks traveling in China about 1,000 years ago encountered this style of painting and brought it back to Japan, where it developed and flourished, both in painting and calligraphy.

Poetry with Sumi-e

Many Asian brush paintings have calligraphy associated with them, often in the form of a poem that describes in words something about the painting. The artist was often a poet as well. One traditional form of poetry that is well known is haiku, a form of Japanese poetry that consists of three lines of five, seven, and five syllables, respectively. Haiku, like sumi-e painting, seeks to capture the essence of an experience or a moment in nature. For example, a haiku that might appear with a picture in this book could be

Shi-Shi holds magic
Sand quivering, rocks rumbling
Sleeping dragons wake.

The Four Treasures

Sumi-e gets its name from the ink that is used for the painting. Traditionally it comes in the form of a flat, often beautifully decorated ink stick (sumi) made from densely packed pine or carbon soot mixed with glue. To make the ink for painting, you carefully grind the stick with a little water in a special ink stone called a *suzuri*, until you get a smooth, black ink of the desired strength. These days it is also possible to buy prepared ink.

The materials of sumi-e are traditionally called the Four Treasures. That's because they are the treasures that help you create a painting that captures the essence of the subject and is full of energy and life. Besides the ink and the ink stone, the two other treasures are the brushes and the special paper. Brushes with bamboo handles are made from a variety of animal hairs; soft ones from sheep or rabbit hair, and stiffer ones from horse, badger, deer, sable, weasel, or other brown animal hairs. A sumi-e painter will use a variety of brushes of different sizes and textures to make a painting. The paper is often called rice paper, but it is actually made from a variety of plant materials, such as mulberry or bamboo.

Seals or Chops

On every painting you will find one or more red seals, or chops. One of the seals is usually the signature of the artist; either the artist's name in Chinese characters or a quality that they feel represents them at that moment, like serenity or happiness. Other chops might be qualities or images meaningful to the artist, perhaps the animal of their birth year in the Chinese zodiac, such as the tiger or the dragon.

Books About Sumi-e

You can learn more about sumi-e. Look for the book *The Boy Who Drew Cats*, by Marcia Hodges. It talks about how sumi-e paintings come to life. Another book that shows you how to do sumi-e painting is *The Sumi-e Book*, by Yolanda Mayhall. And a good way to remember the Shi Shi dragons and think about painting them is with the book *The Dragon Painter*, by Rosie Dickins and John Nez, or *The Sons of the Dragon King*, by Ed Young.

ACTIVITIES FOR THOSE WHO LOVE DRAGONS

Sometimes it's hard to finish an exciting story. You want it to keep on going! Here are some ways to keep the stories of the Shi Shi dragons alive in your imagination.

- Choose your favorite scene from the book and draw it with colored pencils, water colors, or with sumi-e materials. To make a simple sumi-e painting, you might try using black watercolor paint and a pointed brush.

- Make a list of the animals that Jaxon and Allie find in the tide pools. Visit an aquarium and see how many of those creatures you can find.

- What's your favorite game? How would it be different if a dragon wanted to play that game with you? Which rules would have to be changed so that everyone could play?

- If you live near the ocean, visit the beach with an adult and see how many sea creatures you can spot. If you visit a Pacific Northwest beach, you can look for tide pools, and when you find one, look for the creatures mentioned in the story. Treat them kindly!

∴ Choose one part of your favorite dragon, like a wing or the tail. Use bright paper, such as construction paper, to make a pattern of colorful scales like you might see on Shiran or Shalini. (It might take a long time to make an entire dragon, but you could do it!)